THE LAS

THE LAST FIESTA

Andy Rumbold

RedDoor

Published by RedDoor
www.reddoorpublishing.com

© 2015 Andy Rumbold

Previously published in paperback by Thistle Publishing

ISBN 978-1-910453-15-5

Cover design: Rawshock design
Typesetting: www.typesetter.org
Printed in the UK by TJ International, Padstow, Cornwall

To Dad, who never got to read this
and to Mum and María

In memory of Moncho Burgues Mogro

I was trying to learn to write, commencing with the simplest things, and one of the simplest things of all and the most fundamental is violent death.

Ernest Hemingway, *Death In The Afternoon*

Matthew Peter Tassio, a twenty-two-year old student, bled to death in minutes after being gored in the penultimate bull running of San Fermín. Tassio became the first victim of these fiestas, as he sought to live the literary myth created by Ernest Hemingway in his celebrated work, 'Fiesta'.

El País, Friday 14 July 1995

I'd always reckoned talking to the dead was for those close to the edge, or for those who'd already taken the leap. But I don't feel myself near the danger sign, let alone the drop, and yet I had to talk to him. He'd left me with a wide choice of places from around the world where we could start; mostly exotic, dangerous places where he forged his reputation and became a legend. But, try as I might to change the setting, to mix it up a bit as I lay in bed having our imaginary conversations, we always ended up in the same place.

And so I see him in a bar in Cuba, in his last few years, with that white beard, surrounded by fishing friends, sycophants, cigar smoke; alone in his drink. I cut through them all and join him, and wonder what to call him. Mr Hemingway? Ernest? I choose Papa though, because the amount of drink I need to get near to him has given me the courage to be that familiar.

At this point our conversation can go several ways. Maybe he'd ignore me. Maybe he'd cut me down with tongue or fist. Maybe he'd let me in.

I decide on the last option, and we talk. I tell him why I've called him by his nickname, that it somehow brings him closer and makes it harder for me to round on a dead man who can't defend himself. But I also let him know I've listened to him for weeks, months, without him knowing, and now it's his turn. There are things I need to tell him, things he needs to know because unwittingly he had a hand in this too.

I'm not saying he had anything to do with their affair, nor with the carnage that followed. Besides, he didn't even know them; he was dead long before. But it was his book *Fiesta* which prompted Billy to come out here in the first place and head for Pamplona, and for that reason alone, he's involved in this too.

So I buy the drinks, mojitos, one after another, and I tell him the whole thing as he listens patiently, intently. I tell him about their affair, of Billy's ultimate desire to escape and of hers to keep him forever, and how it all ended up in Spain. At last I finish, he nods and I shake his hand. I thank him. I thank him very much. I fight off the urge to hug him, the lovely bastard.

FIVE DAYS TO PAMPLONA JULY 1995

'Got a bit of a limp there, Billy.'

'Yeah.'

He didn't explain.

Even with the limp, I'd recognised him straight away as he stepped out from the customs hall across the black marble floor. He was as lean as ever, tight and defined under a plain white T-shirt, though his blond hair was shorter and the stubble darker. He wore red Converse boots that were faded and scuffed, and strapped to his back was a beaten-up army rucksack.

Eleven years had left few marks. The odd line on his face was sharper now, but those metallic blue eyes were just the same. I put my arm round his shoulder. 'Great to see you again!'

'Yeah. Good to be here.'

'On manoeuvres, are you?' I patted his rucksack.

'That's right,' he said, then smiled. His was a real smile; it almost closed his eyes.

'Good flight?'

He paused for a moment. 'So-so,' he said.

He'd tell me later that week, as we drove back through the Hermida gorge, that he'd nearly turned back at the departure gate because he'd sensed what I'd done. And I can see him now, eyebrows drawn together as he looks out of the window at the trawlers cutting through a choppy Bay of Biscay. I can see the plane banking right and Biscay turning to clear blue skies, and by the time it's levelled out, the bay has been replaced by rolling wooded hills as they make their final approach. I can see Billy looking out of the window again, down at the huge cemetery, row after row of family sepulchres slipping by under him, seconds before landing in Spain.

A long line of yellow and black taxis waited in the sun, like a giant basking snake. We took the one at the front.

There was heavy traffic just outside the airport. 'I think there's a road block up ahead. Probably an ETA thing.'

'Well, we're not in any rush, are we?'

'No,' I said, eyes on the meter.

The taxi driver sighed and lit a cigarette as we crawled forward a few feet before stopping again. The smoke curled up and out of his open window. He mumbled something I didn't catch, but it sounded Basque and negative.

On the hard shoulder, two Guardia Civil were checking out a beaten-up red Citroën 2CV with a Bilbao number plate. One was looking under the dashboard, the other was questioning the driver, who leaned against the car, his arms folded.

Through the road block, we picked up speed. A jet rumbled in the distance, climbing steeply out over the Atlantic. To our right, in the valley below us, factory after factory blew out smoke. Along the river, huge derricks stooped over rusty water.

'So how was Paris?'

'Fine. Didn't sleep too good.'

'Was she nice?'

'There was none of that,' he said, then smiled, his eyes almost closing.

'I don't believe you!'

I couldn't believe he was here in Spain! When he left for the States after school, I didn't think I'd ever see him again. Billy was the sort of person that moved with the world and travelled light, shedding all his old baggage behind him. It always seemed to me that for him, friendships were disposable.

In the city centre, the taxi driver lifted his arm at a boy on a moped with a girl riding pillion. Her crimson hair flowed behind her as they swung stylishly in front of us, just inches off the bumper. They made the lights, we didn't. 'Cabrón!' our driver shouted.

'So what are you up to these days?' I asked.

'This and that.'

I waited for him to expand. At last the lights turned green.

'Such as?'

'Different things.'

We passed the couple on the moped. They'd parked up and were standing on the pavement, kissing. 'Like what?'

'Various stuff.'

He was still annoyingly vague when he wanted to be. Mind you, at school he never really talked about himself much, or his family. I knew his father was a colonel in the US Army and his mother took care of the house back in San Francisco, but not much else. He did tell me once though that his father could be a mean bastard, and that was where the six-inch scar that ran across the base of his back came from.

The bus took us west on the new motorway out of Bilbao, past the factories, the dismal high-rise flats and sprawling suburbs, then around the front of Petronor, a huge oil works, with its twisted mass of tubes and its smoking pipes and flames. At night, all lit up, it takes on an awesome and grotesque beauty.

He fell asleep soon after. I woke him as we reached the bus station in Santander.

'Like I was saying yesterday when you called,' I said in the taxi, as we passed the statue of General Franco too fast to see the red paint of protest on the side of his horse, the spattering of bird shit on his helmet, 'we're going to be meeting up with a few people.'

'So you said.'

'With Simon and Eddy. And Simon's coming out with his fiancée.'

Billy smiled, but his eyes didn't close this time. 'Great,' he said at last. 'I had a feeling it was him.' We slipped along the dark, narrow side streets. The driver drove over some finely broken glass as if it wasn't there. 'What's she like?'

'I've never met her.'

The taxi stopped just past the tiny corner shop on my

street, where the usual group of old men were playing cards, drinking, smoking, shouting under a tired row of hams.

I held the lobby door open for Billy and we climbed the steps then crossed the courtyard. As always, the Airedale on the balcony two floors up started barking. Its bark bounced and echoed off the damp walls.

Three flights of stairs later, I opened the door of my rented flat.

'Let me take your rucksack.'

Billy passed it to me. I was surprised how light it was as I put it on the scuffed parquet floor.

'I didn't realise Simon and Eddy were good friends.'

'They knew each other fairly well.'

'I know he fancied Eddy's sister. Quite fit if I remember right.' He paused for a moment. 'Laura, wasn't it?'

'Lisa.' Quite fit? She was gorgeous. 'I thought it would be good to get Eddy out too.' I had my own reasons for inviting Eddy. Things I needed to know. Things I wasn't going to reveal to Billy, not just then, anyway.

I showed him into the lounge. He didn't seem to notice the crack at the bottom of the glass door, the tape recorder with the play button missing, the tear on the arm of the fake leather cherry red sofa.

He looked out across the bay to the mountains on the other side. 'Nice view.'

I took the compliment personally, like I was somehow responsible for the hills and the sea, like I'd put them there for him to see. 'Smart, isn't it?'

He yawned loudly.

'So if it wasn't a woman, what kept you up?'

'The bed,' he said, still looking out towards the mountains. 'The bed in the hostel was shot.'

I stepped up beside him, respecting the silence, like we were viewing a large canvas in a gallery.

'So are you looking forward to seeing Simon and Eddy again?'

'Of course I am,' he said flatly, at the dirty panes ahead.

As Billy showered, I sat picking at the foam under the tear on the fake leather sofa, wondering why he hadn't seemed that excited about seeing Simon and Eddy again. Billy had stayed several times with Simon in the Easter holiday, down at Simon's parents' place in Hampshire, or at their cottage in Cornwall. And in our final year they'd shared Simon's library of Revolution and Billy's stash of drugs. I imagined lack of contact had pushed them apart. But it didn't worry me. Billy was the magnet who'd draw us all in once more, if only for a week.

The sand was warm as we walked along the crowded beaches past the Magdalena peninsula. What cloud there was, hung high and wispy. A cool breeze from the north had died away the night before and the chances were a south wind was on its way, bringing nothing but dust and hot air for the next few days. They say it drives people crazy if it blows long enough.

'You don't mind me inviting Simon and Eddy along?'

'No.' He shook his head and chuckled.

'You sure?'

'Yeah.'

'I tried getting a few others out, but none of them could make it. Andy Melville's in a forest somewhere in India, trying to save the world. And Paul Turner's just bought a house.'

'And Simon? What's he up to?

'No idea. I imagine he's sitting up some ivory tower somewhere, plotting the Revolution.'

Billy smiled. 'Didn't keep in touch then?'

'No, I haven't seen him since his twenty-first. Didn't even know he had a fiancée. That was the last time I saw Eddy, as well.'

'Could be an interesting week.'

The surf was big for a windless day. We carried on up to the lighthouse and stopped in front of the memorial cross on the edge of the cliff. At the bottom of the cross, a carved stone figure clung desperately to the plinth, looking down in horror at the fall that awaited him.

'What's this about?'

'Republicans pushed some of Franco's supporters off the cliffs here, during the Civil War. It's to commemorate the dead.'

'I thought it was Franco's lot that did that sort of thing.'

'They were all at it. Hard to believe what people will do to each other once you put them in an army.'

We climbed onto the wall by the statue and looked down the craggy cliff face. Waves thundered against rocks below, fine spray rising in thick clouds and falling delicately, like flour exploding from a dropped bag. 'I was in the army, you know?' he finally said.

'Yes?'

'Yeah, I was.'

Even though he came from a military family, it was about the last thing I'd expected. At school he'd found his niche amongst the girls and drink and drugs, and I'd always felt that that lifestyle would stay with Billy for life.

'You're about the last person I'd have imagined in the army, Billy.'

'Well, there you go.' He filled his nostrils with sea air and breathed out through his mouth. 'You must get great surf out here.'

'Yes,' I said, wondering why he'd changed the subject. 'We do.'

We sat out on the terrace of one of the cafés in the main square, a burgundy parasol offering protection from the smothering sun. I held out a packet of Lucky Strikes to Billy. He shook his head. I lit one myself and watched Billy's eyes follow a beautiful girl with silk black hair and a short, hip-hugging skirt crossing the square. The bow-tied waiter came out with two beers and glasses on a tray and placed it on the table.

'Gracias,' I said. I handed Billy the bottle and took one myself. We didn't bother with glasses. 'Cheers, Billy.'

'Cheers.'

'So what made you join the army?'

'Thought I'd do something different, I suppose.'

10

'It's different. That's for sure.'

He sipped his beer, played with the label round the neck of the bottle. 'And what made you come out here?'

'I was working in London doing my Articles and just fancied a change. I decided Law wasn't for me, and I was tired of London.'

'What's that saying? Tired of London, tired of life.'

'There's much more to life than London. Just look around.' Now wasn't the time to reveal the messy stuff, the rotten wood under the paint and filler. Now was a time for the varnish. 'It's beautiful here.'

'Yeah, you've got the life out here, all right.' He looked out across the busy, sun-struck plaza. 'That's what counts.'

'You wait till we get to Pamplona. You've seen nothing yet.'

'So I've heard.'

'Are you going to run then, Billy?'

'No. And you?'

'No chance.' Call it what you want, but I'd already run away from England all the way to Spain. That was enough running for the time being. 'I bet you change your mind.'

'No,' he said. 'No way.'

I didn't believe him though. His love of adventure and his reckless spirit ran too deep. And he had balls, real balls; you could see them in his eyes. I remember going to see The Clash with him once, up in Brixton one holiday, and we were stopped by these four huge black boys. First they asked for a light, then our money.

'We'll settle this down the nearest alleyway if you want,' Billy told them, and you could tell he meant it too.

'You're safe, man,' one of them said, before they walked on past.

I remember thinking 'safe' wouldn't have been the adjective I'd have chosen for Billy. Anything but.

Later on that afternoon in the flat, I got a call from Welsh Richard inviting us to his party that night. It felt good as I hung up. His parties were the ones I wish I could have thrown myself – loud music, a flow of drink, bunches of beautiful women – and as far as Billy was concerned, it would look like I knew a lot of people, had a lot of friends.

The truth of it though was very different. I couldn't speak the language when I first arrived and so I hung around the ex-pat community. It was a mixed bunch, ranging from the interesting and integrated, to the misfits and escapees. Of course the interesting and integrated were normally off doing interesting and integrated things so I hardly got to meet them, and I naturally fell in with the other lot. New country, bars open all night; at five, six, seven in the morning, I'd be hanging around some real bitter losers, pissing my money away.

They soon had him surrounded. Richard's studio flat in the attic was packed, but they still found Billy quickly. He was standing next to the window that looked out over the deserted market with three Spanish girls around him.

'Your friend looks like he's enjoying himself,' Richard said.

'I bet he gets off with Enara tonight.'

'I think the book's closed on that one, mate!'

Enara was exceptionally beautiful, the pick of a very nice bunch. She had deep brown eyes and jet black glossy hair which flowed halfway down her back. She was firm-bodied, her back curved like an unflexed bow. We'd got very close at one point and I'd tried it on.

Enara left the group and inspected the drinks on the table that we were standing next to.

Richard winked at her and tilted his balding head back. 'Having fun, are we?' He nudged her in the ribs with his elbow and laughed. His laughs were fast and infectious, like a machine gun. Enara tried her best to keep a straight face but a trace of a smile broke through. She chose not to answer. Instead she opted for water – cool, bottled agua – before returning to Billy and her friends.

'Lovely, mate. Lovely,' Richard said, eyes on her tanned legs.

'I know.' I thought about all the chances I'd blown through what I was holding in my hand. I lifted the bottle and drank.

The party went on till just past twelve, ending with Richard playing the keyboards and his neighbours downstairs joining in with saucepans on their ceiling. Soon after, some of us headed out to the bars and clubs in town. The place was throbbing, swelled by hordes of Spanish tourists, keen to escape the oppressive heat further south.

A few hours later, a handful of us stepped into 'La Havana', a club with low lighting and crimson walls, which smelt of cheap talc and black tobacco. The music was techno and the dance floor was busy with people moving in minute robotic ways under a strobe, like actors in a silent movie. It was too loud to talk. Enara was trying to though, mouth up at Billy's ear, as they stood on the edge of the dance floor. His head cocked towards her, and he occasionally smiled at whatever she was saying. I felt a tap on my shoulder.

I looked round, saw those glazed eyes, the way they always were before trouble. It was Declan, from Belfast, a rough powerful man with a shock of red hair and a habit of fighting. It would come from nowhere as well, without warning, nothing in the way of a raised voice, or wild gesticulation. But I'd seen enough of his antics to be able to spot it in his eyes.

'All right?' he asked, standing by my side up at the bar. He seemed to think we were friends, just because we were part of the same ex-pat community, just because we happened to share the same language, just because I had spent one night too many with him pissing my money away until daybreak. He too was looking over towards Enara and Billy.

'Yeah. Not too bad. Anyway, see you later,' I said, hoping he'd take the hint.

But he followed me over, pushed his big rounded shoulders between Enara and Billy. She turned her back on him and folded her arms. Billy didn't seem concerned. He looked at Declan and smiled.

Declan turned to Enara. He tapped her on the shoulder and she stiffened. She didn't turn round. He tapped her shoulder again and when she didn't respond, he tried pulling her round to him. Then Billy stepped in. He put his hand between them and moved Declan away, the way a referee does in a boxing bout.

The strobe fractured his movements into tiny jerks, made it seem unreal, as Declan kicked Billy hard in the thigh and swung a hay-maker with his left. Billy ducked out of it. He straightened up and pummelled sharp, venomous fists into Declan's stomach – one, two, three, four times at electrifying speed. Declan fell to his knees. Billy said something to us which I couldn't hear above the noise. He nodded towards the exit as he clutched the top of his thigh, and we left straight away, leaving Declan doubled up on the stained red carpet.

I couldn't sleep that night. The drink and adrenalin were racing through my veins and all I could hear was the beautiful, torturous sound of Enara moaning – they hadn't wasted much time. I'd heard Billy's door close about ten minutes after I'd turned in and I didn't think they'd ever stop. It probably only went on for half an hour or so, but it seemed like all night.

Hearing her made my stomach knot. It reminded me how close they were and I felt envious and alone, like a sailor on a raft at sea cut adrift from his mates. I also felt betrayed by her somehow, as if it were her knife that had severed the rope, even though we'd never got that intimate.

I wondered how many people that night had had sex when they shouldn't have done. Illicit lovers, MDs with their secretaries, or just casual one-night stands. How many people that night had left their stains on strange sheets, on office desks, on car seats, and then returned home to spin stories. Had to work late, darling. It was an exceptionally long dinner; the speech just went on and on. The traffic was terrible. At that moment, the whole world seemed shot through with lies.

FOUR DAYS TO PAMPLONA

It wasn't that Billy lied, more that he chose not to tell you things. Later on that week though, he would open up properly for the first time. We were driving back through the Hermida gorge in the Picos de Europa, on a twisting, narrow road with a vertical drop one side and a sheer wall of rock the other, when he decided to let his secret out. I reckon there was still quite a lot he didn't tell me, but he said enough for me to make at least some sense of what happened that week. I have no idea, of course, what he kept back, but he did recount their final conversation in an English hotel bed, all those years ago when we were still at school, down on the front in Brighton.

'I'm going to lock you up. Stop you from going back,' she said, sitting on top of him, pinning his arms down with her knees. 'Don't think I'm going to let you get away from me that easily.'

'No,' he replied. 'I wouldn't dream of it.'

It wouldn't be long, he thought. Just a couple of weeks. And then he'd be back to the States for good. For better. For the foreseeable future at least.

She released his arms and slid her long legs down alongside his, laying her head on his chest. She'd been doing that a lot of late, he said. After fucking – he admitted he didn't see it as making love; he was never in love with her –

she'd lie there for longer. Normally she was up and dressed in neat, quick movements, seconds after she'd got him to surrender.

'Can I come and see you?'

'I don't think that'd be a good idea.'

She rolled off him and sat on the edge of the bed. 'I see. It's like that, is it?'

'No. I just think it would be a bit complicated, that's all,' he said, looking at her tanned back – at least I imagined it was tanned. In those days she always had a tan.

'It's a big enough country not to be found out in. No one will know.' She turned round, put her hand on his knee. 'Let me sort it out,' she said, then squeezed, smiling too hard. 'We have to.'

For a third day running, I woke to the sound of a drill pounding concrete in the alleyway below. I lay in bed and tried to piece together the night before. I was relieved to find it easy – I had the fight to thank for that. It put back in focus a night which had become blurred, one that was sliding away. I wondered if Enara was still on the other side of the wall. Maybe she'd slipped out earlier to avoid anything awkward. Maybe she had things to do. It was nearly twelve.

Billy and Enara came out of the room at two. His limp was worse, no doubt as a result of Declan's boot, and when he sat down to eat he clutched both sides of the woodworm-ridden table before lowering himself into the chair. We didn't talk much. Six hands tore at crusty bread, teaspoons clinked on mugs. I apologised to Billy for what had happened the night before because I felt guilty; Declan was an acquaintance after all, a fellow ex-pat.

'Forget it,' he said.

'Do you want a hand with the washing up?' Enara asked, after Billy had hobbled through to the lounge.

'No,' I replied, not looking up from the sink.

I washed the plates and cups and glasses, three, four times longer than I normally did. I swept then mopped the kitchen floor, scrubbed specks of fat from the frying pan off the kettle and the tiles on the wall. I chiselled grunge out of corners with a fish slice. Then I went outside onto my balcony, a thin tiled strip too narrow to sit in that faced the courtyard. I smoked a Lucky Strike, barked back at the Airedale on the balcony below. I smoked another. And eventually I went through to the lounge because I sensed each extra minute made my absence more obvious.

When she finally left, she had Billy's address in her hand. And after I opened the door for her, she hugged me and told me to be careful.

'Of what?' I asked.

'Of San Fermín.'

'Why?'

'Porque sí. Es muy fuerte. Bestial.'

'She says it's a very hard-hitting fiesta. We need to be careful,' I explained to Billy. I wasn't sure if she was referring to the bulls or the booze.

'Sure.'

'I'm not frightened of bulls,' I told her in Spanish, swishing an imaginary cape.

Enara smiled at me with worried eyes.

I went back to the kitchen and waited, inspecting the kettle and wall, as they said their farewells on my doorstep.

As we walked through the back streets to the car rental depot, I felt lifted. It was a relief to escape the sordid hole I'd dug for myself in Santander and it was great to be with Billy again; it was as if by sharing the same air, I'd caught a bit of his aura. I'd followed his example and packed a light rucksack. Like him I didn't want to be weighed down by excess baggage.

Billy was lying back in the front seat of our rented Fiat Uno with his bad leg stretched out on the dashboard. It would be a beautiful evening; clear skies, and the sun – rich and full as a perfect yolk – was on its syrupy slide behind us.

'Where we headed again?'

'San Sebastián, to meet the others. Then on to Pamplona.'

We drove on past the turn-off to Solares, with sweeping hills of patchwork greens, where forests interrupt pasture the green of snooker baize, to our left, right and up ahead.

'So, how did it go with Enara?' I finally asked.

'Good. I'll spare you the details.'

And though I was curious, I also didn't want to know. 'Thanks. You know her name means "swallow" in Basque? As in the bird,' I added.

Billy smiled. 'She said she was from the Basque country. That's where we're going, isn't it?'

'Yes. Did she tell you why she moved to Santander?'

'No.'

I was pleased she hadn't offered up such personal details to him so easily, given all of herself away after just a night. So I told him her story.

Enara's mother had died of leukaemia when she was three and she was brought up by her father and her two elder brothers in a small flat, in the industrial and radical town of Rentería. Her father and her brothers were staunch ETA sympathisers. But she wasn't, and they argued long and hard about it until one day she asked them if they'd be prepared to kill for the cause. And they all said yes, without hesitation. So the next day she packed her bags and moved to Santander. That was eight years ago now and it was the last time she'd had any contact with them. And it made me realise the Basque problem wasn't just a national issue, about a separate state from Spain; it could also be a family issue, that divided blood as well.

I reached for my Lucky Strikes on the dashboard by Billy's foot and lit one up. I had a drag and blew the smoke out of my window. I wondered if she'd told him about my shitty attempt to get her into bed. I got aggressive once, after we'd kissed and she turned down an invitation back to my flat. I was drunk, very drunk, and she was drinking water. I only have a smudged recollection of it, but I remember overturning a table in the bar and storming out.

'How did you meet her?'

'Richard knew her, and a group of us went up the mountains for a long weekend. On the second day everyone was tired and just wanted to do a short walk, but Enara was up for a longer one. So we went off together and ended up going on an eight-hour hike. Got on really well.'

I thought about that weekend and a couple of other times the pair of us had gone off walking. And all the other times I'd headed for the mountains on my own, or with other people. Those memories were like little golden capsules, suspended in a pool of booze.

'Got a girlfriend back in the States?'

'No.'

'Just one-night stands these days?'

'Not even that.'

I chucked the cigarette butt out of the window. I couldn't imagine Billy celibate. And I was sure – and still am – it was him operating against the forces of nature and not the other way round. Women would have definitely been interested. And there was nothing he could do about it.

Billy unwrapped some gum and stared down at the huge curving stretch of sandy beach in Laredo. I thought back to our time at school, to a stonier beach. 'You know when you used to go off to Brighton on your own at weekends? Were you seeing someone?'

'No.'

'Johnny Cope said he saw you coming out of a hotel on the front once.'

'And?'

'Come on, you were seeing someone, weren't you?'

'So what if I was?'

'Go on. Who was it?'

'Just someone I met.'

At the time I had no idea who she was, but I see her now, in that hotel bed in Brighton. I see the tanned back. Those long legs. The long dark hair and emerald eyes.

'So how long did that go on for?'

'A while.'

'Where did you meet her?'

'God, Dan. What is this? The fucking Spanish Inquisition or something?'

'Sorry,' I said. 'Look over there.'

To our right, high up out over the huge, rugged headland of Monte Candina, vultures circled and glided above the coastline.

I had a small block of hash which I'd got for the trip in my Lucky Strike packet and I told Billy to roll one up, anticipating he still liked a smoke. His fingers worked skilfully as he folded the paper over the tobacco and hash.

'You still smoke a lot?' I asked.

'Not much these days. Sort of left it in the army.'

'I still find it hard to imagine you in the army, Billy. Why did you join?'

'You're not starting the inquisition again, are you?'

'No, no.' I looked across at his well-crafted joint. 'You haven't forgotten how to skin up.'

'It's like riding a bike.'

He passed me the joint to light.

'No, you go ahead.'

He lit up and the thick sweet scent crept through the car.

'This isn't how I imagined Spain.'

'Were you expecting flamenco and oranges?'

'Something like that.'

The modern motorway we were on sliced through lush green hills and valleys.

'With the odd donkey and Ennio Morricone score thrown in for good measure?'

Billy whistled the score of 'The Good, The Bad and The Ugly'. 'What's your brother doing with himself now?'

I followed his train of thought easily. My brother, two years above us at school, had a poster of the film in his room. But he wasn't the good, nor the ugly.

'He's a merchant banker.'

He paused. 'Has he been out here?'

'No. I haven't spoken to him for a while. We had a bit of a disagreement.'

Billy looked across like he was expecting me to carry on, but I made it clear by my mirror work I had traffic to attend to, cars to pass.

'Hey, Billy,' I said, once there was enough traffic between us and our last conversation. 'I hope everyone has a good time on this trip.'

He didn't answer straight away. I looked across at him. His eyes were out at sea. 'Yeah, I'm sure we will.'

We didn't talk much after that and I didn't try to overtake too many cars.

It was a warm evening in San Sebastián. The light was starting to fade, tangerine skies to the west slipping down and turning bloody behind an unruffled Bay of Biscay. 'La Concha' beach, spectacular and serene, impressed me like the first time I'd seen it. The way it sweeps round like a rainbow, with the two big hills either side and that island between them, which stop the Atlantic coming into town on a bad day. At the top of the right-hand hill, as you look at it from the front, there's a huge statue of Christ. At night, its spotlit figure embraces the city.

There were still a few people about, even though we'd missed the hour of the 'paseo'. Young families, small kids holding big hands, frail arms linking old couples, groups of adolescents larking about, and teenage lovers embracing, stroking, kissing, eyes closed, eyes open, oblivious to the rest of the world that passed them by – oh, to have those years again. The teenage girls are stunning, and look so mature, so young. Spain isn't a good country to read *Lolita* in.

Billy was still walking awkwardly. With his army rucksack on his back, he looked like a wounded soldier.

'Your leg OK, Billy?'

'Yeah. I wasn't expecting his boot, nor his fist either for that matter. Fucking jerk.'

'Sorry,' I said.

He stopped and looked me in the eye. 'Can you just stop apologising? It wasn't your fault.'

'Yes,' I said, checking myself just in time.

'Where are we meeting them?' Billy asked, as we carried on along the front.

'The Hotel María Cristina.'

'Do you know where it is?'

'More or less. But I was thinking of finding a place to stay first.'

'You don't want to stay at the same place?'

'I've got an idea it's very pricey.'

We found a cheap, clean hostel with polished wooden floors, in the casco viejo, a stone's throw from the beautiful baroque Santa María church. Two thousand five hundred pesetas a night for a shared room protected by a faded print of the Virgin Mary above the beds. We paid the old lady up front, then headed out to meet them. Five minutes later, we reached the river and their hotel. 'This is it, I think.'

We stood for a moment below its floodlit, Belle Époque splendour.

'Jesus.'

'Impressive, isn't it?'

'It's a palace. Whatever happened to Trotsky?'

A young man in an immaculate black suit watched us all the way as we crossed the empty lobby, under chandeliers, past thick marble columns and extravagant flower arrangements. Even though my shirt was clean and my jeans were new, they'd got creased in my rucksack. Billy was still in his T-shirt, jeans and Converses, and the shadow had thickened across his face.

'We've come to meet some guests,' I explained in Spanish

to the young man on reception – I felt he and his suit needed an explanation, the way he smiled at us with probing eyes, the way his buttons shone our way.

'What's the name?'

'Webb.'

He called their room; there was no reply. Then he checked their pigeon-hole. 'Are you Daniel Willis?'

'Sí.'

He handed me a note.

'They're in the bar,' I told Billy, before turning to the receptionist. 'Gracias.'

'You're welcome,' he replied in English.

I looked around to try and spot the bar.

'It's that way,' the receptionist said, pointing to our left, his telepathy clearly as sharp as his suit.

The bar had the feel of a bygone era. The tables were mahogany and shone, the waiters wore bow ties and solemn faces, and the sofas and chairs were button-tufted in green leather. An old man sat with a woman at least half his age in one corner, and a group of Japanese men sat in the other. And in armchairs just across from the bar Eddy Roberts was sitting with a very attractive woman in a burgundy dress. There was a bottle of champagne in an ice bucket and three empty flutes on their table.

'Great to see you both,' he said, pushing himself out of his chair. We hugged, then he shook Billy's hand vigorously and slapped his back. He'd lost none of that sparkle round the eyes, and despite the weight he'd put on, his face was still beautiful, so well proportioned. It was impossible to escape Lisa whenever I saw him. He introduced us to Fi, Simon's fiancée.

'I've heard a lot about you both,' she said.

'Only good things I hope,' Billy replied.

She smiled at him, swept her shoulder-length blonde hair back.

'And where's Simon?' I asked.

'He went up to the room,' Eddy said.

A while later, a man with thick black hair stood at the entrance of the bar and surveyed what was in front of him. He raised the stub end of a thick cigar to his lips and drew on it. Smoke plumed out, masking him. When it cleared I looked again. Then I realised. He'd lost a lot of weight and his year-round tan – from skiing in the Alps and Cornish sun – had paled into a patchy white and red. The navy polo shirt he wore hung too far off his shoulders, half a size too big, as he walked over to the table.

'Hello, Dan. Good to see you.' His tone was flatter, more serious than I was expecting. After all, we hadn't seen each other in years.

'Great to see you too, Simon!' I said, then stood up and shook his hand.

'It's been a long time. Hello, Billy.'

'Hello Simon.' Billy stood up too, shook hands then sat back down.

Simon stubbed his cigar out in the ashtray. He got the attention of a waiter and ordered another bottle of champagne and two more glasses. We all sat down.

The waiter opened the bottle by our table and poured it out.

'Here's to a great trip,' Eddy said.

We all clinked glasses and drank.

'So life's treating you well, then?' Simon asked me.

'Yes, pretty good.'

'And you're a teacher now?'

'That's right.'

'Enjoying it?'

'Yes.'

I didn't want to tell him the truth of it, that I'd stopped working for the summer and I wanted to pack it all in. Instead I told him a pack of lies about wanting to start my own school and all the business executives I was teaching because I thought it sounded more impressive than telling him I was working for someone else, teaching young kids, with no chance of progressing beyond the classroom. And even though I didn't see much in my little blister of worry, I remember noticing Simon shuffling in his seat, biting the skin around his nails. 'Good for you,' he said. 'And Billy. What about you?'

He broke away from his conversation. 'Sorry?'

'What are you up to now?' Simon looked quickly at the nail on his right index finger and began to nibble at it before looking back at him. The skin around his nails had gone in places, showing tiny strips of flesh.

Billy scratched his stubble. 'Nothing much. Came out of the army a while back.'

'Really? You were in the army?'

'Yeah. It turned out to be the easy option in the end.'

'I'd hardly call it that.'

'Maybe not. It was just the way things panned out. And what do you do now?'

'Advertising.'

'Oh yeah? Like it?'

'Yes, I love it.'

'Tell me about it,' Fi told Billy. She rolled her pale blue eyes towards the ceiling. 'I hardly ever see him during the week.'

She couldn't have minded that much though, I remember thinking. Late hours had helped to feather what was obviously a very nice nest, if this hotel was anything to go by.

'It's addictive,' Simon said.

'Gave up on Trotsky, then?' Billy asked.

'Yes. Sad but true.'

Billy yawned and covered his mouth with his fist.

'Late night, was it?' Eddy asked.

'Fairly.'

'He was later than me, anyway,' I pointed out.

'Say no more,' Eddy added. 'Was she nice?'

'Very,' I said. 'A friend of mine.'

Eddy chuckled and shook his head. 'Same old Billy. That's very impressive. First night and a result.'

Fi smiled. Simon nibbled at the skin around his nails as he looked at Billy. Billy looked back at Simon. His deadpan expression suggested he didn't appreciate the accolades. 'What area of advertising are you in?' he asked.

'TV commercials.'

'What are you working on at the moment?' I asked.

'We've just signed a contract with one of the big oil companies,' he said. 'I'll be starting on that when I get back.'

Billy tipped his champagne back in one. Everyone noticed. It was almost a full flute. He stood up and burped. 'Pardon me. Where are the toilets round here?'

'Through those doors on the left,' Simon told him.

'Are you in advertising as well?' I asked.

She didn't answer. She watched Billy limp out of the room as she raised the flute to her lips.

'Fi, Dan was asking you something.'

She looked across at me, pulled her dress towards her crossed knee. 'Sorry? What were you saying, Dan?'

We were at the bottom of the steps outside the hotel when the receptionist called Fi back to speak to Simon. He'd been sorting something out at reception when we left the building.

'Shit, it's hot tonight,' Eddy said, wiping the sweat from his forehead with a red silk handkerchief. 'It's so bloody still.'

The river rippled and flowed slowly towards the sea.

'There's a south wind on the way,' I said. 'Then it really will be hot. Meant to drive everyone crazy.'

Billy smiled. 'As if we aren't already,' he said.

A few minutes later, Fi returned.

'Simon's not very well, I'm afraid. He's not coming out.'

She sounded flustered and her eyes darted between us and all around without fixing on anything.

'Do you want to stay here?' I asked. 'If he's not feeling –'

'No, no. I want to go out.'

We ate dinner on our feet, in the old part, up at the bar of one of the many places that was brimming with people and pinchos. Fi appeared distracted at first. Her smile seemed forced and several times she sneaked glances at her watch. It took a few glasses of Rioja to properly relax her.

I remember Eddy being very impressed with the food. He was a journalist who specialised in restaurant reviews, and he'd write about the food in San Sebastián when he got back. I also remember Billy looking at Fi slightly too often, catching her eye occasionally.

After dinner, we strolled along the promenade. The hands of the clock on the town hall pointed to twenty to twelve. On either side of the clock, from the feet of the domed towers, a Basque and a Spanish flag stirred. The building looked very impressive lit up at night, like a palace, easier to imagine royal beds inside than filing cabinets and function rooms.

There was a strong smell of fish as we got nearer the small harbour, tucked behind the eastern hillside, away from dangerous seas. Ahead, the moored-up fishing boats bobbed gently up and down, moving sideways, squeezing old car tyres against the weathered wall. Billy leaned against the esplanade railings and looked out across the bay towards the front.

'Such a beautiful city, isn't it?' Fi said, stopping beside him.

'Yeah,' Billy said.

'I could spend hours watching the light playing on the water.' They stood silently for half a minute or so, gazing out over the bay. 'You know, it's really good to meet some different school friends of Simon's. I've met a few of them and whenever they all get together, it's as if they've never left.'

'He's very different from when I knew him,' Billy said.

'Really?'

Billy nodded. 'Used to be a communist at school. Had posters of Che Guevara and Trotsky on his walls. Cigar smokers were the enemy back then, apart from Guevara and Castro.'

'He told me he was a communist for a while.'

'He once made a hammer and sickle from red card, and placed it on the altar in chapel, before a Sunday service,' I said. 'Funny thing was no one seemed to notice until halfway through the service when the 'Internationale' came blaring out from a tape recorder he'd placed round the back.'

'God. I'm surprised he didn't get expelled for it.'

'No one could prove it was him,' I said. 'He'd delayed the tape. I think there was about forty minutes-worth of blank tape before it came on. Timed to perfection as well. Pure chance. Everyone was praying at the time.'

'The priest was scurrying around at the back of the altar like a beetle trying to turn the thing off.'

I started laughing. 'It was hysterical!'

'And they never found out it was him?' Mouth ajar, Fi looked both surprised and amused.

'No,' Billy said.

'They knew it was him though. He just denied it. Told them he thought it might have been someone from the Brighton Communists he was connected to. They didn't pursue it. He was going out with one of the masters' daughters at the time. Emily Griffin. I think that helped his cause.'

'I've met Emily. I hadn't heard that story before.' And the way she said it, I knew it was something she'd bring up later with him, maybe end up arguing about – not for what he'd done with a hammer and sickle or with Emily Griffin but because there were other people in the world that knew aspects of his life better than she did. He hadn't shared everything. It was as if he'd given her his diary, the most intimate gift she cherished, which she now realised had pages missing. 'What other secrets do you know of?'

Billy paused for a moment. 'No more really,' he said.

We listened to the ends of the sea lapping at the shore for a bit.

'Where did you two meet?' Billy asked.

'At a charity ball for wounded war veterans. After Simon left Oxford. Someone we both knew lost his legs out in the Gulf.'

Billy cleared his throat. 'I was out there too.'

She turned to look at him. 'Really? It must have been awful.'

'It had its moments.' His eyes stayed on the water, on the soft rhythmic waves.

'Well at least you came back in one piece.'

He didn't answer straight away. 'More or less,' he finally said.

We said goodnight to Eddy and Fi on the edge of the old quarter, after arranging to meet them at half ten the next morning. I managed to persuade Billy to come for a beer and we found a dimly lit place with dark red walls and loud music that I made out to be Kiko Veneno's *Me siento en la cama*. The place was busy, but we got a couple of stools at the bar.

'So what do you think of Fi?'

'Nice.'

'Simon's struck lucky there all right. Lucky bastard.'

'Yeah. What does she do?'

'Physiotherapist. You might be able to get her to look at your leg.'

'I'm not sure that would be a good idea.'

'Why not?'

He scratched his stubble, sipped his beer. 'It just wouldn't.'

'He looks so different though, doesn't he? I nearly didn't recognise him. What was up with him tonight anyway?'

Billy reached for my Lucky Strikes and lit one up. He didn't answer.

'I thought you'd given up.'

'I had.'

'Did he look ill to you?'

'No idea, Dan.'

The way he dismissed it made me think he didn't really want to talk about it. 'What do you reckon on a night out in San Sebastián, then?'

'I like it.'

'It's a great place. Great food, great women. It's got the lot.'

He looked me right in the eye and smiled. He still had that uncanny talent of prising out the darker picture with just a look.

I drank some more beer and lit a cigarette. 'I don't know though. I've got this... I don't know how to put it really... this ...' I put my hand on my chest. 'This black space in there somewhere.'

His eyes were still on me, like he knew me so much better than I knew myself. 'A nice Spanish girl would probably sort you out.'

I really wanted to believe him. But I doubted it somehow. I thought of Lisa just then and how Eddy reminded me so much of her. 'I hope so.'

I signalled to the barman and two fresh bottles of Mahou appeared in front of us on the black marble bar top.

'I don't want any more,' he said.

'Go on, one more.'

'No.'

'Just one more.'

'How many fucking times have I got to tell you?' he snapped. 'I don't want another beer.'

'All right. Calm down.'

'You know what? I'll see you later.' He got off his stool and headed out of the door. I remained on mine and started on one of the beers.

There are significant chunks missing from the rest of the night. I remember Billy slapping me in the face, telling me to get up, and one of the barmen looking on behind him. I remember having a close-up, sideways view of all the cigarette butts and discarded serviettes, and wondering where the hell I was. But I don't remember getting there in the first place, nor what else I had to drink beyond that first whisky after Billy had left the bar.

I have a slight recollection of Billy holding me up as I staggered out of the bar, long twisted faces watching on, but only the start of our zigzagged journey back to the hostel.

Not impressive I know, but there's no point lying, pretending I'm someone that I'm not, as if I'm Hemingway himself. I imagine he'd have handled it very differently. He'd have remained calmly on his stool as Billy returned. He'd have drunk at least double what I could manage with no signs of collapse. He'd have been in control, his eyes alert to his surroundings. Somehow I see him eating pistachios. He wouldn't be drinking beer though. He'd be on something far more exotic. A mojito perhaps, or a daiquiri. There was a glamour and sophistication that surrounded him and his drink. Pernod in Paris, vermouth in Venice, fine wine wherever he went. I think of all those bars he helped immortalise: La Floridita in Havana, Harry's Bar in Venice, The Ritz in Paris, to name but a few. And of course the drink they named after him, the 'Papa Doble'. Yes, there's no doubt about it; his life was a heady, high-class cocktail. He wouldn't have been found rolling around in the cigarette butts and discarded serviettes in a run-of-the-mill bar in San Sebastián, that's for sure.

THREE DAYS TO PAMPLONA

I can see her clearly, in black lace lingerie and suspenders, standing in the doorway of the en-suite, the light behind her cutting out a dark figure in sharp relief against the bathroom wall. Her eyes smile anxiously as Billy unwraps the gift she has left for him on top of the perfectly made bed. They have just got back from a weekend in Amsterdam and Billy should be back at school for Sunday evening chapel, but she's insisted that they return to Brighton, to that hotel, for just an hour, she promises. His protests from the airport were half-hearted, but sincere; she took them as a sign of desire.

He unwraps the many layers of shiny gold paper from the present and looks at her from time to time, noticing her awkwardness in the doorway. He tries to smile but he knows that whatever he finds beneath the gold paper will compromise him and weigh him down; that a clean, fast getaway will be that much harder.

The black lace is new and shiny. It firms her long thighs and pushes her breasts out. She lifts an arm and rests it behind her head. Her left leg is bent slightly, and her foot is up against the door frame; it's a provocative pose. Billy keeps unwrapping, wondering when this gold paper will end.

He reaches a black leather box and opens it. Inside is a silver watch. He looks more closely. An Omega watch.

'Do you like it?' she asks, as he hasn't said anything.

'It's lovely, but I can't accept it.'

'Yes you can. And you will. Put it on.'

Reluctantly he pulls it from the box. She tells him to look at its back. 'Forever yours. L' the engraving reads.

She comes across to the bed, takes the watch from him and slips it over his wrist. She fastens the metallic chain link strap, then runs a hand through his hair, across his chest, down between his legs.

'You won't forget me, will you?' she asks as she moves up and down, on top of him, her eyes closing from time to time.

'No.'

'Never?'

'Never.'

'I'm going to buy a ticket to the States.' She loses her focus. Her eyes close again. She moans softly. 'And show you a time you'll never forget.'

'Please don't.'

She rolls off him, moodily.

'It's just too risky,' he explains, although that isn't the real reason. She is starting to get desperate and clingy as they always did with him and it almost always spelt trouble. But this time the stakes are higher. He could get into serious trouble.

'Trust me, no one is going to find out.'

Closing the toilet door behind me, I stumbled down the creaky corridor, then fell back onto the bed. I picked up

Billy's watch from off the bedside table. It was still the one he had from school. A silver Omega. We all asked where he'd got it from, coming back one long weekend with it suddenly strapped to his wrist, but he never told us. Looking at it closely for the first time, I noticed an engraving on the back. 'Forever yours. L', it said. The time was five thirty.

I couldn't get back off to sleep again properly, as dark grey light crept through the gaps in the shutters and my body still buzzed with booze. Instead I dozed, and dreamt right on the surface. I was down at Simon's parents' holiday cottage in Cornwall. I didn't place it as the Easter holiday I'd spent with Simon and Eddy, when we were fifteen, but they were both there. And we walked along the cliffs, as we did that holiday. Out to sea, I could see something huge rolling towards us. I realised very soon what it was. 'Tidal wave,' I shouted. We turned and ran. Billy and Simon were fast out of sight but I was stuck to the spot, trying as hard as I could to run. When I looked round again, it was no longer a tidal wave but an avalanche almost on top of me and before I knew it, my dream went white.

I was up just before nine, disturbed by some prolonged hammering upstairs, and had a long shower. I left Billy a note saying I was going out and would be back in an hour or so.

The paving stones were still damp and smelt fresh and bleachy from the cleaning buggies that had washed and scrubbed them in the early hours. A beggar was sitting on the steps of the Santa María church waiting for the worshippers and tourists to drop coins into his cardboard box on their way through the doors. A priest slid past him and went in, as if he wasn't there.

Up above, between the dark narrow streets, the sky was a rich blue. It was going to be another hot one. I sensed it would be another windless day, waiting for the one from the south to arrive.

I wandered along the promenade all the way round to the other side of the bay. The tide was out and a few people were strolling along the beach. A group of boys were playing football down towards the water's edge. I felt surprisingly good; I'd somehow managed to slip from the grasp of the temples-in-a-vice hangover I deserved.

When I got off the promenade, I went to a café, sat on the terrace and watched the immaculate, measured women walk by. I ordered a coffee and picked up a copy of *El País* on the table next to me. As usual, 'Caso GAL' news made the front page, a clandestine war waged against ETA since the late eighties by an organisation calling itself 'Grupos Anti-Terroristas de Liberación' – GAL – the full extent of which was now coming to light. There had been secret executions of ETA members and supporters in forests and allegations of a huge cover-up involving senior figures in the PSOE Government.

I was about to pay up when I spotted Eddy, on his own. I called him over. This was my chance.

'Good morning, Dan.'

He took a seat.

'Sleep well?' I asked.

'Yes thanks. I raided the mini-bar again though, when I got back. Didn't feel too good first thing. Did you carry on much longer last night?'

'Not really,' I lied.

'Any sign of life from Billy?'

'No.'

The waiter came over to the table and I ordered two white coffees.

'Didn't John Toshack manage the team from San Sebastián?'

'Yes he did. Real Sociedad.'

'What's he up to now?'

'Busy turning a very good Deportivo de la Coruña side into a pretty average one.'

'You know I'm now a football manager of sorts,' Eddy said. 'I organise the Old Boys' tours. Last year we went to Portugal and this year we're trying to get something together for Italy.'

'All the old crew?'

'Yes.' The waiter arrived with the coffees on a tray. Eddy leant forward, looked me in the eye. 'Your brother came last year.'

'Shame I couldn't make it.'

'We did talk about it. He said he had to follow his heart.'

'His sentiments always were so fucking noble.'

'You know they've got a baby?'

'Yes.'

'A baby boy.'

'Check out the girl in the red top.' A stunning girl in a

43

red T-shirt and a denim skirt walked by. As good a reason as any to get off the topic. Eddy turned to look.

'Very nice.' His eyes lingered on her tanned legs and then they were back on me. 'Lisa hoped to see you at the christening, you know?'

'Couldn't make it. Busy that weekend. Big football match on TV.'

'Oh well.'

I struggled briefly with dual urges, both wanting and not wanting to know. 'So what's she doing with herself? Professional mother now, I suppose.'

'She's not actually. She's in an orchestra, set up by a friend of hers. Ex-London Symphony Orchestra or something.'

'She must be pleased then. She always wanted to play professionally.'

'Yes, she is. I think Rob wants her to give it up, though. He doesn't think it's too good for the baby to be brought up by a nanny.'

'Do you get on well with him?'

'Not too bad.' Eddy dropped his tone. 'To be honest though, Dan, I'd have preferred you as a brother-in-law. She often said it was the hardest decision she ever had to make in her life. She loved you, you know?'

'Well, that's nice to know.'

'Didn't you get any of her letters? She said she wrote you loads.'

'No, never opened them. Binned them on sight. Anyway, a part of me is pleased they're married.'

'Are you really?'

'Yeah, I am.'

'For you or them?'

There was no point lying to him. 'For me. It meant I could let go. Before they married, I'd always clung to the idea she might, just might, possibly come back.'

'Well, it's all behind you now, Dan. Let bygones be bygones, hey?'

We had another coffee, and I tried to talk about something else, anything else, rather than what we'd been talking about.

Eddy then went off towards the promenade and I walked back towards the hostel. The smell of bleach on the paving stones had gone now, replaced by living smells, the whiff of coffee and tobacco coming out of bars, and fish and garlic and olive oil coming from the maestros' kitchens, as they prepared the day's pinchos. The beggar was still there on the steps of the church, on his feet now, box out, as the devout began to trickle through the doors. And one of those that walked past him into the church was Simon.

I stopped, nearly called out, but instead I followed him. Inside it was dark and cool and the sweet smell of frankincense hung heavy in the air. Simon walked down the nave, towards the altar. He reached the rails at the front and got down on his knees. Then he bowed his head, as if in prayer.

I couldn't believe what I was seeing. At school we'd had a belly full of church in a huge Neo-Gothic chapel high on a hill, and Simon was one of a handful who refused to take any part. In fact, Simon and Billy were the handful's two first fingers, index and middle. They wouldn't go up for communion, they wouldn't sing the hymns, and when it came to prayer, they stuck out defiant and offensive, like those fingers do. Amongst five hundred or so kneeling bodies, the handful sat impassively, impressively, heads up, not tails. And there was nothing the masters could do about it. From their pews they rolled discouraging eyes, taking mental notes of trouble, of those that refused to bend. But there was nothing they could do to the handful, at least not when it came to making them pray.

In a couple, it was a weekly act of rebellion. Robert Brookes and Ric Steyning were both desperately trying to be punks at the time, even though they'd got the wrong decade. But that wasn't the case with Billy and Simon. For Simon it was to do with his politics. For Billy, it wasn't so much a political thing – his politics were nowhere nearly as well defined as Simon's. He just simply didn't believe in God.

Simon crossed himself then stood up. I walked out fast, before he saw me, and waited outside for him just beyond reach of the beggar.

'Good morning, Simon. Feeling better?'

'Yes, thanks. Just admiring this church.' The morning threw cruel light on his skin, sharper contrasts of red and white. He looked surprised to see me, and a little uncomfortable. 'What time are we meant to be meeting?'

'Ten thirty. What are you reading?' I asked, noticing the book in his left hand, down by his side.

'Hemingway. *Fiesta*. I thought it would get me in the mood for Pamplona.'

'Nearly through it?'

'I'm at the bit where they go up into the mountains. Which reminds me. I forgot to ask yesterday. Could we go up to the mountains for a couple of days? I've heard the Picos de Europa are stunning. I've brought my boots out, just in case.'

'I don't see why not,' I said, thinking we would be going away from Pamplona, but happy enough with the idea. 'Let's just run it past everyone.'

'Sure.'

'I didn't realise you were into hiking, Simon.'

'I'm not really. It's just something I need to do for work. We're looking for a location for an advert, and the Picos de Europa came up. I'd like to check them out.'

Billy was wetting his razor in the basin when I let myself into the room. He had a towel round his waist and his hair was wet.

'Did you sleep well?' I asked.

'Not too bad.' He looked at me in the mirror with his chin up as he dragged the blade through foam, along his jaw line. 'Head all right?'

'Yes. How's the leg this morning?' I asked.

'Better. Nice out?'

'Lovely. Bumped into Eddy. Had a coffee together.'

'Still catching up on old times?'

'Yes,' I said. 'Old times. I saw Simon as well. You know what? I think he's become religious. I saw him praying in a church.'

Billy stopped shaving, dropped his razor in the basin. 'No way.'

'I know.'

'Jesus,' he mumbled, then splashed his face and wiped it with a towel.

'He wants to go up the mountains for a few days. What do you think?'

'Why not?' he said, still bent over and drying his face. I noticed the six-inch scar that ran across the base of his back. The one his father had given him with a belt once, for throwing his dinner on the floor. 'It might do us all some good,' he added.

Later on that week, as we rounded yet another blind rocky corner on the right side and away from the drop, back through the Hermida gorge, I'd learn how badly he'd fallen out with his father. He told me he didn't want his inheritance – he referred to it as 'that blood-stained will' – and after leaving the war, Billy wrote to him from a military hospital on the east coast and told him so, but he didn't hear back. He said the silence stank; even then he wouldn't grant him his wish for no more than a clean break, for nothing more than nothing. He wouldn't even give him that.

Army behind him, he took a bus back to San Francisco, all he possessed in the world on his back. Through the pines on the edge of the Presidio he could see home. A light was on in the kitchen. His mother was preparing the dinner. A figure came out onto the porch, drink in hand, and sat in the rocking chair. Billy watched him lull forwards and backwards, sipping at regular intervals. Then he turned his back on his father and headed away from the woods, to the pseudo-hippy houses on Haight-Ashbury; Day-Glo commercial, a front for the tourists. His older brother lived just off the main drag. Billy rang the bell.

'You look terrible,' his brother told him. His opening line from the threshold.

'What do you expect? I've been in a war, not a bloody health farm.'

And he told me of the bits of broken Arabic they'd learnt, that slid from his mind alarmingly fast. The huge stark gut of the C-141 – loaded with vehicles, and soldiers along the sides and miles of twisted wire underfoot – seemingly impossible to get off the ground. The view from the rear cargo doors at 2:00 am, in a cold and windy Dhahran, of silhouetted bombs attached to a row of F-16s – how that brought it home that it was for real. The continual reflex wiping of the lenses on his gas mask in the compound, to keep his mind off darker thoughts. The sleep-punctured nights of SCUD alerts. And the brief which was meant to turn them into real men within hours – a number of them were excited by what would happen to them in the most apprehensive, shit-inducing way he'd ever encountered; it all meant nothing, I think, compared to the slightest squeeze of that trigger, gun on the boy who ran for his life.

We left San Sebastián at one, Simon, Fi and Eddy following in their rented black Seat, and we made a detour via

Guernica. Coming off the motorway, we snaked our way down the hill on the narrow country road between the trees and the depleted river. Now and then there was a reminder that this beautiful land was also a troubled land as we'd go under a bridge or pass a road sign, which was invariably daubed with ETA or Herri Batasuna graffiti. It didn't seem to fit somehow, the running spray paint of hard-line politics woven into such beauty.

There wasn't much to see in Guernica. What they'd rebuilt after the bombs were mostly soulless grey blocks, but we still saw the tree up by the parliament building and the Henry Moore statue in the park in memory of all those civilians killed by the Luftwaffe on that sunny market day.

Back on the motorway, I thought about the weekend I'd had with Lisa in Madrid, where we'd seen Picasso's painting of Guernica in the Reina Sofia, and she'd patiently explained it all to me, where we'd got beautifully drunk together in the packed bars around Santa Ana, where in a hotel room on the Gran Vía at five in the morning she told me that she loved me.

Then I thought about what Eddy had told me the day before. I knew they had a baby. My mum had told me. After that I put the barriers up. I didn't intend telling Billy about it. But I'm not very good at keeping things to myself.

And so I told him about Lisa, the gorgeous girl in my life for three years who went on to marry my brother. That I couldn't compete with the bastard and his Oxford degree, his cricket blue. How I packed in my Articles as soon as I found out they were getting married and packed my bags, coming straight out to Spain. Of course I missed the wedding, and my mother was upset about it, but what could they expect?

'How did it come about?'

'She came up to stay one summer at my dad's when we were at university. I had a job in this bar in the evening and I think she and my brother spent a lot of time together then.' A couple of minutes of silence slid by before I carried on, as crudely buried fragments of our final weeks and days together, and the months that followed, resurfaced. 'She broke down in tears on me in bed. Told me she didn't love me any more, but it wasn't because there was someone else. And I believed her as well because I'd always thought she was honest. Then about three months later, she phoned me up and said we had to meet. I thought she was going to say she wanted to get back together again. I couldn't wait. So we went out for dinner and she told me. I just got up and walked out. Didn't even think to ask her if it had started before we split up.'

'At least she was straight with you.'

'I know. At least she had the guts to tell me. Unlike my brother. But that was how it worked out. I thought I was going mad. Lying there at night thinking about them, knowing there was nothing I could do. They've got a kid now, you know?'

Billy was silent for a moment. I looked across and saw him running his hand up and down his jaw, like he was rubbing the information in. 'See. If you'd married her, that would have been you done and dusted. You'd be a nappy-changing lawyer.'

I forced a laugh out and felt the goose pimples sprout from the back of my neck and surge upwards, touched by Billy's kindness rather than tender thoughts of nappy changing.

'That's true,' I said. We drove on for a bit in silence and my hair settled back down. 'Everyone's married or getting married these days.'

'Seems that way.'

'Yes. We don't want to get left on the shelf though, do we?'

'Dan, you're only twenty-nine. What have you got to be worried about? You've got plenty of time. The pair of us have. Plenty of time.'

'Doesn't it ever bother you?'

'Why should it?'

We were back on the Bilbao by-pass now. The sharp blue sky had paled in a haze of smoke. Below us to our right, the curved titanium panels of the nearly completed Guggenheim gave off a velvet sheen. The rusted river flowed slowly past it through the heart of the city, like corrupted blood.

'Do you want to meet up with Enara later then?' I asked.

'No.' He paused for a moment. 'You know, I think you need to be open with her, Dan. Tell her how you feel.'

'Maybe.'

He looked at his watch.

'What's the time?'

'Just gone three.'

I remembered the engraving. 'Hey, Billy. Who's the 'L' on the bottom of your watch? Who is she?'

'Someone you never knew,' he lied.

We coasted along gentle sweeps of fresh motorway for a while, silent. I was thinking how much I'd just told Billy about Lisa and how little he was willing to tell me. It was all very well for him to dish out advice on being open, and how I should show my feelings. But when it came to himself, he wasn't prepared to do the same. And it made me feel exposed and resentful.

I now understand why Billy wanted to tell someone, anyone, especially in the beginning. The glow he must have felt, his dark joy – and, just possibly, his guilt.

And I can understand why he didn't tell me, and why the illicit secret had to remain theirs. But I wanted to know, so I'd push him for details back through the gorge. And to be fair to him, he gave me them.

Waiting for her to pick him up, sometimes bound for the country, sometimes for the airport. Checking in separately, seats rows apart, then the hint of a smile that united and promised things to come as he caught her eye, walking down the aisle. The single room and the double they took, to put suspecting receptionists off the scent, all part of a game they played to increase the thrill, the fear of being caught, even when they knew they were safe. The triumph of finally lying on the huge expanse of bed in the double, with its sparkling tiled bathroom, knowing that this was their prize, their fortress for the night. The unslept bed in the single the next morning, miniature soap still wrapped; the tousled sheets in the double, undone by sweat and sex.

These scenes were the bricks in their secret building of thrill, of fear.

Gradually though, the excitement would dull, turn routine, and with it, what he felt for her. He began to feel sorry for her – she couldn't see he wasn't so keen any more – as she went about planning their reunions with evergreen gusto. Yet with that pity, I sensed a contempt. He despised her for not seeing what was happening or, worse, not wanting to see.

I hadn't really wanted them to see my flat, not after seeing their hotel in San Sebastián, but Eddy needed the toilet and I needed to make a couple of calls. I noticed all sorts of dirt just then that I'd previously been satisfied didn't exist. I'd cleaned the kitchen, the bathroom and swept the floors for when Billy had come out. But I hadn't bothered getting out the furniture polish or cleaning the grubby marks off from round the light switches and door handles, and now the flat appeared to me in a new light. Clearly shabby.

I remember Simon's eyes scanning the living room, picking out the missed cobwebs, the cracked glass in the door, the cassette player without the play button, no doubt. I know there was no way of telling, but I reckon he was thinking I'd definitely missed out somewhere along the line, if this was the best I could do. To cap it all, Fi spotted a cockroach in the bathroom, something she probably wouldn't have announced, except that she yelled sharply.

'It's beautiful,' Fi said, standing on the patio of the hotel Real, five star, high up on the hill, looking out to the mountains of Liérganes on the other side of the bay. 'What a place.'

'Well, Simon wanted the best. And this is it.'

We looked in silence for a few moments at the mountains and bay.

'You know,' Simon said, 'I'm sure I recognise this hotel from somewhere.' His eyes narrowed, as though he was trying hard to recall a memory, as he scanned the picture before him.

'Yeah?' Billy asked.

'Yes,' he said, eyes still facing the bay, squinting less now. 'There's something familiar about it.'

We went to reception, and I wrote down directions to a fish restaurant for them, where we were to meet for dinner at half nine. I asked the receptionist if she could tell the taxi driver as well. She nodded and gave me that model five-star smile, cosmetically perfect if not quite meant, learnt and remembered from her days on the five-star training course, no doubt.

The flats in the barrio pesquero are run down, dirty grey paint flaking off damp walls, and the restaurants don't look much, but the food is out of this world. We waited for them outside the poshest one. It had fishing nets on the ceiling and the lighting wasn't as stark as in the other places, nor were the walls bleach white. The other places had a certain charm, unceremonious service, and the food was just as good, but I thought Simon, Fi and Eddy would prefer the atmosphere in the one I'd chosen.

When the others arrived we took a table by the window away from the glass tank where you could watch your dinner walk, if you were having crab or lobster, before it arrived boiled on your plate. The place was busy for so early in the week. There were no empty tables.

'So when are you getting married?' Billy asked her.

'We haven't set a date.' She looked lovely, out of her jeans and into a thin-strapped slate blue dress. She was wearing make-up, delicately applied round her eyelashes and eyebrows which highlighted her pale blue irises. Her lips were subtly redder. 'A long way off, I imagine.'

Simon picked at the skin around his index finger. 'Who knows? It may be sooner than you think.'

She paid no attention to his remarks. 'So is there anyone close to being a Mrs Wyatt?' she asked.

'No.'

'A girlfriend?'

'Not even that.'

She sipped her white wine, still looking at him, and impressed a faint red print of her bottom lip around the rim of the glass.

'Let's get a bottle of iced water, shall we?' Simon said to me. 'It's quite hot in here.'

'Good idea,' Eddy said.

After the meal, when the brandies arrived, Simon reached into his jacket pocket and handed us each a Montecristo, then a cheroot for Fi. He lay back in his seat and lit up, the smoke curling softly, slowly upwards. He looked more relaxed now, but there were still little tight knots pulling around his eyes and jaw. It was hard to see where the stress came from. He had a very well-paid, interesting job, a house in Fulham – a house, not a rented flat – and a beautiful fiancée. A world more than I had, at any rate.

At school, we all seemed to be in the same boat. The gap hadn't appeared that big. Now there was an ocean between us. Our only common link, a shared but shrinking chunk of adolescence. I bet he'd never pissed his money away, sloshed his way round the bars and beyond until daybreak. It would never have even occurred to him. This English teaching bit was a sham. It hid my low life, covered it with a sheet of respectability and in his presence I felt like a cheap fake.

We took two cabs into the centre of town to the Plaza Cañadio. It's one of the smartest squares in Santander and a popular haunt for the beautiful crowd. In the summer it's packed, the bars spill out into the square, and that's where we ended up. I wasn't sure if I'd take them up the hill, to the more radical, alternative bars where I felt more comfortable and where political persuasions count for more than Lacoste polo shirts and perfect teeth. I'd see how things panned out.

A couple of drinks later, we crossed the square and went up the hill.

The smell of hash was strong. The narrow, poorly lit street was busy with teenagers drunk on Kalimocho. A spiky-haired lad was bent double, throwing up on the pavement as a girl rubbed his back. A foot away another lad was skinning up, seemingly unaware of the vomit. And just up from him, a couple kissed and fondled in a doorway, oblivious to any worlds outside theirs. We weaved our way through and up.

Just as we were passing the Iguana, a raucous bar near the top of the hill well known for its drugs and punk music, the swing doors banged open.

'Hey, yank. I want a word with you.'

We all stopped and turned round. It was Declan, the Irishman that Billy had put on the floor in the nightclub. Billy smiled, walked back down towards him as if he was greeting an old friend.

'Watch it, Billy,' I called out.

'Don't worry. He's not going to do anything. Are you, buddy?'

Declan answered him with a fist. Billy managed to dodge it and then held onto his arm. They wrestled each other to the ground and rolled a few feet down the hill. And before we had time to do anything, Billy had him face down in an arm lock.

'Get the fuck off me, you cunt! I'll fucking kill you!' Declan yelled.

'I'm not letting go until you've calmed down. And don't make me do anything you'll regret.'

He tried desperately with his free arm to unpin himself. Beaten, he pulled on Billy's shirt.

'Declan, just leave it!' I said.

Seconds later, Billy let go of him. We were right behind him now.

Declan stood up and dusted his shirt down, his chest heaving as he caught his breath. 'I'll come and find you,' he said to Billy, menace in his velvet Irish voice. 'When you're least expecting me.'

Billy stared at him with cold eyes. 'Feel free. I'll even give you my address if you want. What's the number, Dan?'

'I know where you live,' Declan said to me.

'I can't wait for your visit,' Billy told him.

'I'll be seeing you,' he said, before he staggered back towards the Iguana. 'Mark my words.'

I quickened my step, worried that Declan might re-emerge with a broken bottle or some other weapon intended for Billy. I'd seen knives before in the Iguana – used mainly for cutting the hash, but easy enough for Declan to get his hands on and use for his own bloody ends. So I was relieved when we finally stepped over the threshold of the Rubicon bar. Not that we were totally safe there – Declan knew I drank there – but I knew enough people in the Rubicon to say hello to, to at least feel a semblance of protection. Inside, the light revealed a trickle of blood running down Billy's cheek.

'You're bleeding,' Fi said.

'It's nothing,' Billy replied. He wiped the blood away with the back of his hand.

'Qué le ha pasado a tu amigo, Dan?' Moncho, the owner, asked as he played dice up at the bar with Pedro. As the last word slipped through his grey, walrus moustache, he peered over his round wire-rim glasses to get a better look.

I explained the business with Declan.

'Hijo de puta!' Pedro said.

Fi went off to the toilet and came back with a tissue which she used to clean up his wound. Moncho poured out a glass of orujo and gestured to Fi what to do with it. She dipped the tissue in it then put it to Billy's cheek. He didn't flinch as she applied the alcohol.

'How do you know him?' she asked, still dabbing.

He swept her words away with the back of his blood-stained hand. 'I don't want to talk about it.'

'You don't have to speak to her like that.'

'Stop it, Simon. Can't you see he's shaken up?'

'I'm not shaken up,' Billy added. 'I just don't want to talk about it, that's all.'

'OK,' Fi said, smiling so warmly at him that, for the briefest of moments, I saw her giving away her most primitive heart to Billy, not Simon.

We sat at the table nearest the door, underneath the huge poster of Hemingway that Moncho had on the wall. It was a portrait of him in his later years, in a thick woolly jumper and a glass in hand. His contented look gave no clues to what he'd later do to himself.

The door opened. A man held it for a woman and they stepped inside.

'I like this place,' Eddy said, as if he sensed I was worried and was trying to distract me.

'It takes me back a bit,' Simon said, looking at the posters advertising the Cuban Castro night Moncho was having later in the week.

'So how come you gave up on it all?' Billy asked, twisting the straw in his mojito.

'What? You mean my politics?'

'Yeah.'

'I just lost my faith in human nature, I suppose, I mean the more idealistic view of it.' He paused for a moment, still looking at Billy. Billy was focused on the tabletop. 'Certain things happened to shake my faith in human nature. In the end, I agreed with Hobbes more than Rousseau, I suppose.'

I nodded, remembering very little about either of them.

'Hobbes more than Rousseau,' he repeated, eyes still on Billy.

And then Fi nudged him.

I remember it quite clearly although it wasn't that obvious, just a slight twitch of the elbow. And for a second, I sensed real tension in the way she did it, the way he stared at Billy, the way Billy stared at the tabletop.

'Trust me, will you?' he said to Fi, under his breath. He looked across at Billy and me. He cleared his throat then sipped his mojito. 'So are you ready for the Picos de Europa?'

'Yeah. I didn't realise you were keen on the mountains,' Billy said.

'I'm not really. I'm just checking it out to see if it's suitable.'

Billy ran his fingers across the wound. 'Suitable?'

'For an advert. We'll have to see if it fits the bill.'

'What's the advert?' he asked, inspecting his fingers; no blood.

'For a petrol company. They want a greener image. And mountains are as good a place as any to start.'

Billy shook his head and smiled.

'Something the matter?' Simon asked.

'Not a damn thing.' He stood up and searched his pockets. 'Fuck it. I've lost the keys. I think they must have come out on the road back there. Can you lend me yours?'

'Sure. You're not going yet though, are you?'

'Yeah.'

'But we've only just got here,' Eddy told him. 'And you've hardly touched your mojito.'

'I don't want it.'

I handed him the keys. 'Leave them under the mat. Are you all right?'

He shot me a look and I remembered I shouldn't have asked.

'We'll come with you,' Fi said.

'I'm not worried about a prick like that.' He walked towards the door.

'Tomorrow,' Eddy shouted. 'See you tomorrow.'

Billy didn't reply. He put a hand up to Moncho and Pedro as he left.

There was an awkward silence which Eddy broke. 'What was all that about?'

'I don't know,' I replied.

Fi stood up. 'I think someone should go with him,' she said.

'Sit down!' Simon snapped, and for the first time ever I witnessed a sharp flash of the master in him. 'I think he just wants to be left alone,' he added softly. 'That's all.'

'And who are you to be bloody ordering me around?!' she said, not sitting down. Instead she marched up to the bar and ordered a large brandy from Moncho, and she drank it in one.

We soon got on to the fight. I was quick to explain the small, ex-pat world that linked me to Declan, that nothing but a shared language – I didn't mention the drinking – had brought us together for a very brief past.

Then we made our excuses to each other – and to ourselves, no doubt.

'It all happened so fast,' I said. 'We didn't even have time to help him.'

Simon nodded.

I'm not sure Fi was convinced. She sat silently, watching us, with traces of the earlier storm still on her face. And though I can only speak for myself, I think we all felt ashamed for not acting in the street, as we stood and watched, mesmerised by the violence.

We left the Rubicon at about one. I put the others into a taxi and walked back to my flat. There were still plenty of bars open at that time and I was tempted to stop for a last one but I managed to check myself. The way I was feeling, one would have turned into ten.

I let myself in with the key under the mat. Billy was still

up, in his room. Through the frosted glass I could see him walking about. I knocked on the door.

'Hang on.'

A few seconds later he opened the door just enough to stick his head out.

'Do you want a beer?' I asked.

'OK.'

In the lounge, we exhausted the topic of Declan in a handful of words. He didn't want to talk about it.

'That was so embarrassing earlier when they came back here,' I said, as I brought two more beers through.

He was rubbing his eyes, sitting on the edge of the chaise longue. 'Why worry about it?'

'Easier said than done though. That bloody cockroach.'

'Well, at least it wasn't a rat.'

I couldn't tell if he was joking or not. 'I don't think they were very impressed.'

He stopped rubbing. 'Oh, fuck that! Who cares what they think? This is your place and this is the way you live. You don't have to justify that to anyone. For fuck's sake, man!'

I put the TV on before taking a seat in one of my fake leather cherry red armchairs. Pepe Navarro was interviewing a transvestite prostitute on *Cruzando el Mississippi*. I wasn't really listening.

I finished my beer and went to bed. I left Billy watching my favourite Spanish film on video – *Jamón, Jamón* – with English subtitles, starring Javier Bardem and Penelope Cruz. It's a dark, very funny parody of Spanish macho culture. Naked bullfighting at midnight, à la Juan Belmonte.

Although I was shattered, I couldn't get to sleep. I started off with Billy's snappy mood. At school he'd always had a sharp switch of temper – but generally against those who took advantage of their seniority to be rude or unfair. But I couldn't remember an inoffensive confession ever setting him off. And I put it down to his scrap with Declan. Then I wondered what Simon, Fi and Eddy must have made of it, of me really. After all, it wasn't as if Declan was a total stranger and I knew that connection, however tenuous, cast the spotlight of guilt my way, or, at the very least, shaded their inaction more than it did mine. Maybe even exonerated it.

And then there was the cockroach. I could hear Fi and Simon talking just then, in a pristine, five-star bed.

'Disgusting, it really was.'

'Oh don't worry, darling. We're not staying there, are we?'

'No, thank God.'

I bet the Hotel Real didn't have cockroaches scurrying across their toilet floors.

But at least they didn't get to see the real dirt. Me, drunk out of my head, in the 'clubs' with flashing neon signs, that everyone knew were really brothels, up on the hill near the prison.

Someone else got to see it though. And not just anyone else.

It was the last time I went. I heard a voice pulling me back as I climbed the hill. I knew straight away who it was. I stopped but didn't turn round. And she stepped round in front of me. 'Please, Dan. Don't go.'

She draped her arms over my shoulders and I kissed her. Then my drunken hands fumbled over her breasts and down between her legs. 'No.' And she pulled my wrist away and stepped back. 'Believe it or not, there are women who can see some good in you, you know?'

'Oh yes? Like who?'

She didn't answer. Just stared at me – and I tried to kiss her again. She offered me soft eyes and lips, but not her mouth. And I felt so full of boozed-up frustration, I gave up and walked straight past her, up the hill. I didn't look round, but I knew Enara was still there, eyes on my back. And I didn't go with a prostitute that night. Instead, I sat on the kerb outside one of the clubs and cried my eyes out.

The first few times I went, I tried to look for excuses; before and after – but never during. I blamed my actions on Lisa. It was her fault. She'd driven me to it. As for the sex itself, I tried to justify it in utilitarian terms, we were both getting what we wanted – the prostitute got the money, I got the sex – and so it satisfied the criteria of the greatest happiness for the greatest number. But after a while I realised utilitarianism didn't really work for morality – at least not sexual morality anyway – the way it judges consequences rather than intentions. It's not difficult to see really but it took me a while. I mean, I knew this girl at university who told me she slept with this guy once because he'd worn her out with his efforts and in the end she just gave in, just for a bit of peace and quiet. His happiness, or gratification, was greater than her reluctance. Fine in utilitarian terms, but it still didn't justify it.

As the drink surged through me, I felt invincible as I headed for the suspendered girls in thickly perfumed clubs. The money in my pocket gunned down the possibility of getting too close. This was a transaction and I knew I could get what I wanted without the fear of getting hurt. It was so easy, and yes, it was a turn on. Sitting up there at the bar, knowing you could have whoever you wanted, whenever you wanted. And all because of money, the power it gives you. Absolutely no ties, no broken hearts. Just uncomplicated sex. And yet after it was over, the very feelings that attracted me there in the first place would always turn against me. I'd always end up feeling sick with myself – choked by overwhelming remorse and perfume – and emptied. Emptied by the clinical, business-like nature of what we'd done and how we'd done it. I never learnt.

But it didn't stop me going and after a while I started to worry I was getting hooked. I knew it had nothing to do with Lisa now. I'd been too often to continue blaming her, and anyway I enjoyed it, even though I didn't like to think where it might lead, to lonely mackintoshed wanderings through Soho or somewhere, to the back seats of seedy sex cinemas, to the slippery floored booths of peep shows. I thought about having therapy when I returned to England one summer, but I never went. I have enough trouble trying to establish the real motives for my own actions as it is, so I don't know how anyone else can. Besides, I didn't want to spend a fortune for some glib woolly liberal explanation that it was to do with not being breastfed or how I hadn't listened to whale music in the womb or something.

So I decided to try and sort it out myself. It's getting better slowly. I'm trying to learn how to get back in touch. To get close again.

I'm not sure why – probably because of what happened in Pamplona – but the other day I equated my fear of getting too close to women with that of the matador towards the bull. The good one, the brave one, the artist – so they say – gets as close as possible, tries to be at one with the bull. The bad one, the coward, the cowboy, avoids getting close and risks far less. It's easy enough to see the parallels.

The last thing I remember before falling asleep was Lisa and my brother, Lisa and the baby, Lisa and me. It could have been my baby, that. It could have been me that was changing the nappies, singing the lullabies. And I would have tucked him up, kissed him goodnight and not come home drunk. Was that daunting? Could I have handled that? Yes, I could. I would have given her a baby. And it would have been the most beautiful baby in the world.

TWO DAYS TO PAMPLONA

It was just before five when I heard the click of the front door. I'm normally quite a deep sleeper, and it was closed very quietly, as though not to disturb anyone, but it still woke me.

I lay there for a moment, before switching on the lamp on the bedside table and getting out of bed. I coughed loudly, twice, although I didn't need to. I stood by my door for a minute or so, listening. I strained to hear things, creaking floorboards, imagined I heard things, realised for a second I was just imagining them.

I walked down the hall, tense, turned lights on, expecting him to spring out of the dark at any moment from one of the rooms, lounge or kitchen. But there was no Declan. Just a note on the kitchen table and a set of keys.

Five minutes later, as he was about to walk through the tunnel going to the bus station, I caught up with him.

'Billy, where the fuck are you going?' I asked, trying to catch my breath.

'I don't know yet. Down south probably.'

'What the hell are you doing? What's going on?'

'I just need some time and space to myself.'

'It's nothing to do with last night and Declan, is it?'

'No.'

'Well, what's happened all of a sudden then?'

'Nothing. I just need a bit of space, that's all. Besides, as I said, I'll be back in a couple of weeks.'

'Oh great! And what the hell am I going to tell the others? Billy's decided to go off for a bit?'

He pulled at the shoulder straps on his rucksack, readjusting the weight, then straightened his back. 'Tell them I'll be in touch.'

'Well thanks, Billy. Thanks a fucking million!'

I turned round and started marching back to my flat. Twenty yards on I stopped and looked back, expecting, hoping Billy would still be there, or following me. But he'd disappeared through the tunnel.

And as I walked back up the hill, to the sounds of soft cooing from pigeons resting high above in the nooks of weathered roofs, I wondered if his sudden departure might have had something to do with Fi. Maybe he knew what would happen if he stayed, as if he sensed an irresistible force pulling them together, something carnal, primal, that cut through all other bonds, including those of engagement. And the anger I'd previously felt towards him gave way to surprise, then respect – I'd never imagined morals featured much in Billy's thinking regarding the opposite sex and I viewed his decision to leave as a very honourable one.

An hour and a half later I was woken by my intercom.

'I've changed my mind,' he said, as I opened the door. 'I think I need some sleep.'

We walked across the fresh, marble-floored lobby of the Hotel Real where a different receptionist with the same five-star smile phoned through to their rooms, but they weren't there. She told us to look in the lounge area or in the garden. We eventually found them on the patio sitting round a table in the sun.

'Did you sleep well?' I asked Fi.

She looked tired – darker, slightly narrower eyes that dimmed those pale blue circles – and didn't manage a smile. 'Not particularly, no.'

'It was quite hot last night, wasn't it?' I said, knowing they would have had air-conditioning in their room, and also knowing that her body language towards Simon was cool in her lack of eye contact with him, in those frosty shoulders and folded arms.

'We've been admiring that house over there,' Simon said, not giving her time to reply.

The house he was referring to always reminded me of a fairy-tale castle, with its little pencil turrets, tucked away amongst the trees.

'It wasn't that hot. We had the air-conditioning on.' She was swinging a crossed leg, arms still locked, looking well away from her fiancé.

'Right,' I said.

'It's like something out of a brothers Grimm tale,' Simon said.

'That's Emilio Botín's house,' I replied, slightly disorientated by the tandem conversations I was having. 'Owner of the Banco Santander. His daughter's married to Seve Ballesteros.'

I pointed across the bay to Pedreña, to where the couple

had a house, next to the golf course that Seve had grown up on. Pine-lined fairways, and built around a hill. It always looked immaculate from the little ferry boat that chugged over to Somo, stopping in Pedreña on its way out and back.

'I should have brought my clubs out.' Simon looked at Billy. 'Yes, I know. Another bourgeois pursuit, I'm afraid.'

'I kind of like golf myself actually.'

'We'll have to have a round sometime. If you're ever in England, or I come over to the States.'

'Yeah,' Billy nodded, and that real smile broke through. The charming, disarming one. The one that mended worlds. 'I'd really like that, Simon.'

'Me too.'

'Is everyone all packed and ready then?' I asked.

'Well I'm packed but I'm not sure I'm ready for this,' Eddy said.

Simon stood up and looked out over the bay. 'You know, I finally recalled last night where I know this hotel from. I think my parents stayed here. They sent me a postcard.'

Billy turned away from the view to Simon. 'Yeah?'

'Yes. Back in the good old days.'

'Come on,' Fi said, sounding impatient.

Simon looked out for a second or two longer. 'Back in the good old days,' he repeated, like he was talking to himself, before he turned round and followed us inside.

It was in a Californian motel, not a five-star hotel, along a straight dusty road dotted with cactus trees, close to the Mexican border, that Billy understood the full extent of her possessiveness and her potential for destruction. She'd insisted on stopping there, the first place, anywhere would do, and behind closed doors had forced herself upon him straight away to wipe clean, he believed, the memory of that lunchtime bitch. Then they started drinking heavily in their sunless room, and the argument they'd had earlier in their rented Chevrolet reignited over the blonde teenage waitress in the diner who had flirted with Billy the moment he walked in. He was accused of doing nothing to discourage it. In fact, his eyes had apparently undressed her as she took their order, and she might as well have walked over with their two dishes in nothing but her black high heels. Then she served Billy's burger and chips before her tuna and avocado salad. 'I'm sorry, Madam,' she said, smiling pure sex at Billy as she placed the other plate on the table.

'Bullshit,' he replied, as a counter to her continued accusations in the motel room.

When he slammed the door behind him, and walked past the faded, frameless prints of flamenco dancers that lined the corridor walls, half a bottle of tequila remained on his bedside table. By the time he returned nearly an hour later, the bottle was by her side and empty. She lay naked, asleep, covered by a white sheet. Next to her was the strap to Billy's Omega, pulled from the watch in what must have been a drunken rage.

We were walking out across the hot, windless car park when the receptionist called out a few yards behind us. 'Excuse me, sir. I think you left this in your room.' She held up a thick, red leatherbound book in the air.

Simon turned round and stopped. 'Oh thank you.'

'You're welcome, sir,' she said, a little out of breath but still managing that five-star smile as she handed him the Holy Bible.

Billy and I had hardly said a word since leaving the hotel. He'd seemed preoccupied with something as we got into the car.

'That's where we're going,' I pointed out, finally breaking forty minutes of silence. I knew that what he saw to the right of him would change his focus of attention, whatever it was he was thinking about. Jagged snow-capped peaks cut clean through the broken, vanquished cloud.

'Great.' He turned round to look at the others, a safe braking distance behind us, then smiled. 'I bet Eddy's wondering what he's let himself in for.'

We crossed the bridge in San Vicente de la Barquera – to our left, the estuary dotted with fishing boats, to our right, harbour and sea – and then climbed the twisting road out of town, past the monastery on the opposite hillside.

I thought of Simon coming out of the church in San Sebastián and about the Bible handed to him in the hotel car park. It ran counter to everything I thought I knew about him and what he stood for. I wondered what had caused his conversion from a Trotskyite atheist to a capitalist Christian. Time alone surely wouldn't have exacted such a change. There had to be more to it than that.

'What do you reckon has caused Simon to become religious?' I asked.

'Who knows?'

'Bloody odd though, isn't it? Don't you think?'

He didn't reply, so I carried on. 'He seemed a bit pensive as we left, didn't he? I wonder what he meant about his parents staying there "back in the good old days".'

'No idea.'

We drove on in silence for a while.

'"Back in the good old days" to me says they're not like that any more.'

From the corner of my eye, I saw him shaking his head. I heard him sigh. 'I think you're analysing things too much, Dan. You've still got a fucking lawyer's head on your shoulders, you know? Maybe he just saw that time of his life as a good period, that's all.'

We drove on to Panes and turned left through the Hermida gorge where the mountainsides hang steep over the road, stained with black wet moss, nature's graffiti. High above, mountain goats leapt across the rocky surface at impossible angles. Wire mesh fences at the bottom stopped the scree from sliding onto the road. Further up, the river gushed fast and cold at the rapids. The sun was blocked out now by the steepness of the mountainsides, and the air was fresh and cool.

I was excited now. This was my land, the place I came to escape the sordid mess I'd made for myself in Santander, where I came to feel alive again. It reminded me of Enara now; we'd been up here several times together, before I fucked it all up in Santander. From an empty glass in a packed bar, I'd managed to turn a bond as solid and natural as the rocks we'd stood upon, as we crossed the Picos' stunning terrain in quiet union, into a cheap, distant mirage.

Through the gorge the sun was strong again as we drove on to Potes. I decided not to stop as the town was packed with Germans, and Brits off the ferry, exploring the narrow medieval streets, easy enough to spot in their shorts and socks and sandals. Instead we drove up to the tiny village of Espinama. It was a stunning drive with views of the eastern and central massifs to our right, snow-capped peaks jutting out like giant white pencils.

We parked in the small square and let a livid, purple-faced farmer chase his cow and her calf up the road before we crossed it, to the Fonda Vicente Campo, a family-run hotel with old stone walls and great food.

The three rooms we took were clean and basic, a stone's throw down from the restaurant and bar, next to the cool, rocky stream that would bloat and bellow once more in autumn, when the rains arrived.

The walk I planned would take about three and a half hours. We took the cable car to the top of Fuente Dé, then walked round to Peña Olvidada where the path splits in two and gives the fit walker an option. Left takes you up towards the awesome, haunting world of sharp, craggy summits and nothing green. To a land of exhilarating freedom, where a sense of adventure and danger tingles through your body like that first erotic touch, especially if you're up there on your own. And it can be dangerous – very dangerous if you're walking alone. A misplaced foot and twisted ankle that high can leave you in all sorts of trouble. And then there are the clouds that just sneak in from nowhere, in no time, and in effect render you blind. The right fork's safer, and more trodden. It takes you round behind Peña Vieja, and down towards a sweeping green valley, with wonderful views of the eastern massif ahead. Right is the lyrical route, left the elemental.

Given Eddy's lack of fitness though, I knew we weren't going to have that choice – we'd have to take the route to the valley below – but now we were up here, the lack of option was frustrating. I wanted the prospect of getting up high, with the adrenalin flowing and the fast tunes you conjure from your breath, in time with the most elemental thing of all: the thump of your pounding heartbeat.

Further down we passed the Chalet Real with its steep red roof, once a hunting lodge used by Alfonso XIII, and later on, General Franco.

'Do you do any hunting, Dan?' Simon asked.

I remembered the holiday I had with Simon and Billy down in Cornwall. At night we'd hunt rabbits with Simon's father, the dark silence shattered by the crack of his twelve bore. I always missed, deliberately. 'No. Not my thing, really.'

'And you, Billy?'

'No, not any more.'

'Just women now, is it?'

Billy looked down at his feet and frowned. 'No,' he said.

'I think it's the other way round,' I said, thinking of Enara. 'He lets them hunt him.'

'I'm sure he does.'

And a few seconds later, Billy left us behind and went way on ahead. Watching him go, you could clearly see him limping, but it didn't hold him back.

We sat on the grass and waited for Eddy again by the tiny church that stood alone in the meadow between the eastern and central massifs. The occasional cloud was stretched thin across the sky and from along the valley you could hear the soft dull tap of bells on faraway cows. Billy stood up and walked over to the weathered church doors. They were padlocked.

'So much for God keeping an open house,' he said.

'How does it go?' Simon looked skyward and frowned for a second. '"Ask, and you will receive; seek, and you will find; knock, and the door will be opened".'

Billy knocked on the doors. No answer. He came back and joined us on the grass.

'Isn't that from Revelations?' he asked Simon.

'No. Matthew seven. Sermon on the mount. RE O level, remember?'

'Fuck, no way.' He looked across at Simon. 'You've got a good memory.'

'Yes,' he said. 'I suppose I have.'

'Oh my God! Hello!' Fi said.

A Pyrenean mountain dog had come up behind her and started nuzzling into her groin. The old dog's coat was matted and mucked up with mountain living. It had left the flock of sheep it was guarding nearby, sensing food, no doubt. After cocking an ear and twitching its nostrils, it flopped onto the grass, flat out next to Fi. She stroked its stomach.

'Careful, Fi,' Simon said.

'I have actually stroked a dog before, believe it or not.'

'I know, but it might not be that tame.'

She carried on stroking it, rolling her eyes skyward.

When Eddy finally caught up, at least ten minutes after we'd stopped, his legs bent and he fell backwards onto the grass. His cheeks were red and forehead even redder, where beads of sweat had formed on his brow.

I dug into my bag, soaked a red bandanna in water from the bottle and gave it to him. He sat up, put it to his forehead, then ran it across his cheeks. Veins from his neck rose thick and fast. He had trouble putting the bandanna on so Fi tied it round the back of his head for him.

Billy stood up. 'Ready then?'

'Steady on, Billy,' Eddy said. 'We're not in the army now, you know?'

'Yes, give Eddy a couple of minutes. We're in no rush. We're all right for time, aren't we, Dan?' Simon asked.

'Yes, fine.'

Billy paced about. He looked keen to get going.

'You go ahead,' Simon said. 'I want to take some pictures anyway.'

'Anyone coming?' Billy asked.

'Yes,' Fi replied.

'We'll catch you up,' I said.

As they set off, Simon got his camera out from his backpack. It was a black SLR Nikon, and he spent a good ten minutes snapping away, purely landscapes, for work, he said.

'The right type of place for your advert?' I asked.

'It looks pretty good.'

I had mixed feelings about it though. On the one hand, I felt proud that I'd introduced him to the Picos, that I was in some way connected to the grand process of top-end advertising. On the other hand, I thought it was also exploiting and cheapening these awesome mountains, like a form of sacrilege.

Photos done, we carried on walking. Apart from the dull knock and crunch of soles on stone track, all you could hear was the sound of cow bells and trickling water from the stream which wound its way down next to us.

Looking ahead as we waited for Eddy again, we saw that Fi and Billy had reached a part of the route where the mountains close in on either side and the track twists round steep-faced corners. And soon they were out of sight.

'Where are Billy and Fi?' Eddy asked, when he finally caught up. 'Have we lost them?'

'It seems that way.'

'Up ahead,' I said.

Half an hour later, the views opened up again and we could see a 'pueblo abandonado' of about six cabañas below us. The roofs had caved in on four of them. Two looked as if they were being renovated, probably for summer or weekend retreats, and they weren't far off being ready. To the right, the mountains loomed above the cabañas and straight ahead you could see down into the wooded valley and to the mountains on the other side. And then I saw them.

They stepped out of one of the deserted buildings. Simon stopped, looked confused for a moment, ran the back of his hand across his sweat-covered brow. Fi and Billy carried on walking, apparently not noticing us.

'Hey! Hang on!' Simon shouted, waving at them.

They stopped, turned round, didn't shout or wave back.

When we finally caught up with them, they were sitting on the grass just past the last cabaña.

'What a beautiful place,' Simon said. He looked down at Fi. 'What are they like inside?'

She shook her head. 'Basic,' she said, looking at her feet as she replied.

Simon turned round and walked back up the track. He stood outside the abandoned cabaña they'd just walked out of, looked through a broken window. Then he went inside. Fi kept looking up at the doorless entrance. Billy stared out to the valley below, eyes apparently fixed on nothing as he peeled an orange. Eddy lay out on the grass and covered his face with the bandanna.

'Yes, I see what you mean,' Simon said to her when he finally returned. 'Very basic. It smells as if animals have been in there.'

Past the pueblo abandonado we followed the 4x4 track down through woodland. A viper lay recently squashed by a tyre, its insides squeezed out just below its head. To our right, a bird of prey glided high above us, falling and rising effortlessly before it stopped and hovered. Seconds later, it soared up and away and out of sight. We descended the last forty minutes in silence, a silence which seemed heavy, not from tired limbs, but more likely from wondering if Simon had been alluding to something up by the deserted cabañas.

'You looked like you really enjoyed that today,' Eddy said.

'Um-hum,' Billy said, mouth half full of cheesecake. We were sitting in the restaurant upstairs, next to a middle-aged English couple, who were talking ever so quietly, spooning their soup away from them, cutting small pieces of bread from their side plates. In the far corner a group of eight similar-aged Spanish people were eating properly; sharing dishes and laughing loudly, bread hand-broken on the tablecloth.

Eddy obviously wasn't too well. He couldn't manage his pudding.

'You should get it down you,' Simon said. 'You'll need all your strength for the walk tomorrow.'

Eddy frowned at his flan before looking up at Simon. 'We're not doing another walk tomorrow, are we?'

Simon persuaded Billy and me without any difficulty. 'Fi?' he asked.

'I don't know. I'll see how I feel. I might stay behind with Eddy. My thighs are feeling rather stiff.'

'That's hardly surprising. All that... exercise,' Simon said.

It was the slightest of pauses and he hadn't exaggerated the word in any way, yet Fi looked sharply at him. Billy's eyes moved between the two.

'What?' Simon asked her.

She shook her head and sighed.

'What we could do,' I said, 'is get up early and drive round to the Asturian side of the Picos. There are some lakes up near Covadonga. It's really nice up there. Great walking too. I know a really good refugio where we could stay. It shouldn't be too busy midweek. It's quite basic. Dormitory accommodation, bunk beds. That sort of thing.'

'Just like school,' Eddy said. 'We could run the gauntlet.'

'What's the gauntlet?'

'A sort of initiation ceremony, where you had to run up and down the dormitory while the rest of the boys clobbered you with their pillows,' Simon explained.

'Trouble was, some of the boys would put their army boots inside them and Billy here was expert at tripping you up and then you'd get a real beating on the floor,' I said. 'I got a couple of real hammerings as a result of his tap tackles.'

'Sounds brutal,' Fi said, silk-voiced, slip of a smile at him.

'It was just fooling around really,' he said.

'While they're off walking, Fi, we can get some practice in,' said Eddy.

'I think I might need it.'

I told them they might like to look around the monastery in Covadonga, where legend had it that the Christian reconquest of the Moors began.

'So after bashing the hell out of each other, Eddy and I can get down on our knees and pray for forgiveness.'

'Yes,' Simon said, eyes on Billy. 'We could all use a little prayer, I suppose.'

There was a short silence, which felt uncomfortable, and so I broke it. 'Packed up the atheism with the Marxism then, Simon?'

'No.'

'So what's with the Bible studies?' Billy asked, smirking slightly.

'It's a very recent thing, Billy. Months not years.'

Billy continued to smile, like he was dismissing Simon's words out of hand.

'Oh yes, amusing, isn't it?' He sat forward, put his elbows on the table, linked his nibbled fingers. 'But atheism is just as irrational as believing, Billy. Non-belief has a lot more credence – street cred if you like – what with Sartre and Camus, yet it's just as much a faith, a firm belief. Just a firm belief in nothing, as opposed to something, that's all.'

'Do you not think it's a bit of a cop-out though? Like a comfort blanket.'

'No, not at all, Billy. It's been a real struggle. And I can tell you this much, it's not over yet.'

'So why the hell bother? Surely you either believe or you don't and that's that.'

'Why the hell bother? Because at the heart of it all is forgiveness, something that doesn't come easily to me, Billy, I can assure you, and I'm only just starting out.'

The tall, fair-haired waitress presented us with the bill and five chopitos of orujo on the house and we slammed them. I felt the heat spread fast across the bottom of my throat and down onto my chest. Eddy's eyes bulged as he swallowed. Then we went downstairs to the small bar. Four old men were sitting around drinking, smoking and playing cards. One of them, with erratic teeth and narrow eyes, slammed his fist on the table and swore.

'Look out,' Eddy said. 'Trouble on the way.'

I explained that that was how the Spanish went about things. They could shout at each other, wave their arms about at each other, even trade their worst insults, but nothing ever really came of it. Or very rarely. They just got it out of their system and that was that. That murky undercurrent that draws people so quickly towards violence, where it's all so restrained but you know it could go off at any moment, has a weak pull here.

I know very little about cards, but I'd learnt a few dice games in the bars along the way – I hadn't totally wasted my time drunk – and so I asked them if they wanted to play. They all wanted to, and I got some dice from behind the bar. I showed them a game called 'Mentirosa'.

It's like poker, with full house, three of a kind, that sort of thing. You have to beat what the person next to you passes you. Some of the dice are out on the table but the rest are hidden under the leather cup so you have to decide whether they are bluffing or not. If you don't believe them, you can ask to see them. If they are telling the truth, you get an 'M' to your name but if they're lying, they get the

'M'. Or you can believe them but you have to throw higher for the person next to you. Each time you lose you get an extra letter, until you reach the 'a' in 'Mentirosa', and you're out of the game. The winner's the last one in.

I must have taught them too well because it didn't take long for me to get a 'Men' by my name. At this stage, Simon and Eddy had an 'M', Billy was letterless but Fi had a 'Menti'. And she was getting upset with Simon who came a turn after her, as he kept asking to see her.

'You don't trust me, do you?'

'Not when I know you're lying.'

'I'm not just talking about the game.' Fi sounded slightly drunk.

'We're not going to talk about this now,' he said, raising an index finger. 'OK?'

'Yes, sir,' she said, before saluting him and laughing.

'Look, we're in the middle of a game. Now let's just get on with it, shall we?'

He put the dice in the cup, passed them on, and we carried on playing.

Fi's problem wasn't so much that Simon didn't believe her. It was more that she believed Billy too easily. She never asked to see him, just took his word for it, so when he called 'Full house' and she accepted it, she had no choice but to call 'Four of a kind' on Simon. And her face gave away the fact that Billy bluffed quite often.

'I don't know why I keep believing you,' she said to him, as she looked under the cup, accepting he had three of a kind. 'I'm going to ask to see you next time.' She rolled two of the dice on the table and pushed the cup with the three hidden dice on to Simon. 'Ah! Full house!'

Simon looked at her and smiled. She smiled back and put her head in her hands. He lifted the cup and Fi got an 'r' to her name. Simon rolled, looked quickly at the dice under the cup and passed it on to me. 'A six,' he said.

'Very daring,' I told him and accepted. I took the six out from under the cup, left it out and rolled four in the cup. 'Two sixes,' I said to Eddy.

'Even more daring,' he said and accepted. He looked under the cup and moved another six out. Then he rolled the three dice in the cup and looked under again. 'Three sixes,' Eddy called.

Billy accepted and by the fact that he didn't put the third six out on the table, it was obvious that Eddy had been bluffing. Billy rolled, then he looked under the cup, shielding the dice from Fi. 'Four of a kind.'

He put the cup back over the dice and passed it on to Fi.

She looked for a while at his face, smiling at him, trying to guess from his eyes, from his expression, if he was lying or not. 'I think I want to see you,' she said.

'Any time you like,' Billy said.

She was still looking at him, still smiling. If she started the flirting, then Billy wasn't exactly discouraging it. He smiled back, wide grin on his face, chin resting in his hand.

'I think you're lying,' she said.

'I wouldn't lie to you, Fi.'

'Wouldn't you now?' Her eyes stayed on his as she tilted her head back, her smiling mouth ajar. 'I'm going to lift you.' And then, alternating her gaze between Billy's eyes and the table, she slowly lifted the cup. 'You bastard!'

Under the cup lay two more sixes that made up the poker. Fi laughed. We all laughed. She slapped Billy playfully on the thigh. He grimaced slightly.

'I'm sorry, I didn't mean to slap you that hard.'

'It's all right. It's nothing.'

'That's quite a limp you've got. Ask nicely and she might massage it for you,' Simon said.

'Oh for heaven's sake!' Fi snapped.

'Well you are a physiotherapist.'

'No, you weren't... Oh, let's just leave it, shall we? Remember what Graham said.'

'Do you really have to bring this up now?'

'Well, you started it.'

'All right, all right. I'm sorry, OK?'

'Trust. Remember that word? That's what he said,' she answered, not looking at him, and flustered, by the look of her.

I was lost at this point. Eddy kept his head down and played with the dice, like he was embarrassed to be privy to their conversation. Billy watched Simon and Fi, his chin still resting in his palm.

'I really don't think you're in any position to be looking so bloody smug, Billy. You've got a fucking nerve, you know?'

'Simon, just stop it!'

'Well, he has,' he answered her, as he stared at Billy.

Billy showed his palms, up towards his head. 'Look. Just calm down, yeah? What's your problem?'

'Don't start patronising me, Billy, and pretend you don't know what this is about. For once in your life, show me that respect, at least.'

His palms went up again, fingers splayed this time. 'Of course I respect you, Simon. You know that. Come on.'

Simon took a deep breath and stood up. 'It's been a long day. I'm going to bed.'

Eddy and I said goodnight to him but he hung around for just long enough to show he wanted and expected Fi to go with him.

But Fi didn't move. 'Goodnight,' she said, as he finally left for their room.

'Another orujo?' I asked everyone, after a few silent, lead-weight seconds.

'Yeah, sure,' Billy said.

'I'd love one as well,' Fi added. 'In fact, why don't we just get a bottle of it?'

Billy turned to her and smiled. 'Good idea,' he said.

And so I did.

'How is your leg, by the way?' Fi asked, after we'd slammed the first ones from the new bottle.

'Sore.'

'I can give you a massage if you want.'

'Now there's an offer,' Eddy said, then laughed.

'I am a physiotherapist, Eddy!'

'Not now,' Billy said. 'Maybe later.'

Eddy was the next to turn in, about fifteen minutes after Simon. And then it was my turn, almost an hour later. The bottle was almost empty, just enough left for a couple of shots. I got up and said goodnight and then I too hung around for a second too long, like Simon had, waiting for the pair of them to call it a day as well. Instead Billy poured out the last two orujos.

As I left the bar and walked down the cobbled stone path to the building where our rooms were, I was worried. The combination of Billy and orujo could make a woman do something she might come to regret. Any woman – including an engaged one – who might have had something to do with him already. He somehow managed to tap a reckless vein in people, especially women, and it would just happen. I don't know if he manipulated it or not, my guess is that he didn't, but either way, it was very dangerous. It crossed my mind to go back and have a word with him but, to my shame, I didn't.

ONE DAY TO PAMPLONA

Billy wasn't there when I woke and as the night before came back to me, I began to suspect the worst. I lay in bed, unable to summon the energy to get up. Strips of light slipped through the shutters, painting bright bands on the wall. I didn't attempt to pull them up. Too much light wouldn't have been good for my head. I knew I shouldn't have had those last two orujos. Just as I always knew, every morning after. I looked at my alarm clock on the bedside table. The hands pointed at half past nine and a dog was barking somewhere in the village. Ten minutes later, as more fragments of the night before were coming back, Billy returned. He'd been out running.

'Bloody hell! That's keen of you,' I said from my bed.

Billy started easing his trainers off at the doorway.

'Did you stay up much longer last night?'

'No.'

I sat up, and immediately wished I hadn't. And then I asked him. 'Billy, you haven't... with Fi, have you?'

'No,' he said, as he sat on his bed and began to pull his T-shirt off.

'You promise me?'

'I said no, all right?' he muttered, through cotton.

'That's not the same as a promise, Billy.'

While Billy was in the shower, I heard voices from the room next door. The thick walls sieved out details of what sounded like a fast exchange of heavy words. Only tones got through, but they were consistent enough to let me know that whatever Fi and Simon were saying was very heated, especially to start with, and it wasn't one-sided. They were both shouting. And I imagined it had something to do with a young American, naked just then and out of sight, washing the sweat and dirt off his body, just feet from their door.

I skipped breakfast for a coffee and a cigarette. Only Eddy looked as bad as I felt. His face was still puffy and bags had formed under his eyes. Billy glowed after his run, and Fi was freshly showered, wet hair swept back like fine silk. As for Simon, he was clear-eyed and alert, although his skin was patchier again.

On our way round to the Asturian side of the mountains, we stopped briefly in Potes for Simon to buy some lightweight walking boots. He bought Fi a pair as well, even though she'd decided she wasn't going to be walking with us but would stay with Eddy instead. And he bought her some flowers. Red and white carnations. The colours of San Fermín, I remember thinking, and blood and bandages.

'For last night,' he said. 'And this morning.'

She kissed him quickly on the cheek. 'You didn't have to, you know?'

As we were faced with quite a long drive and kept to the same car arrangements as before, I decided to take advantage of the opportunity to ask Billy a few questions. It must have crept up on me during the morning because along with my hangover, my head throbbed with a strong, clear feeling that things weren't right between Billy and Simon, and that they hadn't been right for a while. That maybe it wasn't just to do with Fi. The peseta was finally dropping. The scene the night before acted as a magnet, pulling in the tension between them, the pointed comments here and there, and the odd look that seemed to cut deep into a secret that only they shared. And now I came to think about it, Billy had seemed uptight when I surprised him with the news that Simon was coming over. All these things were now starting to come together and form into a coherent bundle in my brain, labelled 'Billy and Simon = trouble brewing'.

'What's going on between you and Simon then?' I asked, as I overtook a lorry on a long freshly tarmacked stretch just outside of Potes, knowing Simon wouldn't have any trouble overtaking as well.

'I guess we're pretty different now.'

'Yes.' I sighed. My foot on the pedal had pumped me up. 'I'm sure you are. But it still doesn't explain a bloody thing. Look, I know it's none of my business, but I wouldn't mind knowing what the hell's going on.'

Billy put his feet up on the dashboard. 'It's a long story, Dan.'

'Well, it's a long way to Covadonga. You've got plenty of time to tell it, if you want to.'

Billy reached for my cigarettes on the dashboard and lit

one. 'This is sort of difficult to say.' He dragged hard on the cigarette a couple of times, as if it was the end of a spliff. 'What the hell? You know I used to stay with him at Easter?'

'Yes.'

'Well, things sort of… happened.'

'Oh yes? Like what?'

'Just things, you know?'

'No, I don't bloody know.' The runaround treatment was starting to irritate me now and I put my foot down again, this time in protest and with no traffic to pass. I think he picked up on it.

'All right.' He flicked his ash out of the window. 'Hope you're ready for this.'

'Yes, go on,' I said. We were about to go back through the Hermida gorge. The sun closed out and the air cooled.

'Well, I had an affair with his mother.'

I eased off the accelerator. I needed to concentrate. The combination of my speed and his revelation would probably have caused an accident. 'You're fucking joking! When did all this happen?'

'In the sixth form.'

I remember seeing Simon's mother for the first time when she came to drop him off at school in her five-series BMW. It was at the end of the Christmas holidays in our first year. And she left a strong impression. She was quite tall with a good figure, buxom but not fat. She was certainly striking, great posture, with straight black hair which just brushed her shoulders. And she had a suntan in winter. She must have been mid to late forties at that point and she looked very good on it. Simon later told me she'd done some modelling back in the sixties and it didn't take much imagination to picture her twenty-five years younger, a few pounds slimmer, smouldering through the pages of *Vogue*. Age had been kind to her. At least it hadn't exacted much in the way of metamorphosis. And yes, I had fantasised about her, on my own, at night.

'So how did it come about?' We reached the narrow, twisting roads, blind corners one side, sheer drops the other, and I was taking it good and slow. I looked in the mirror. Simon, Eddy and Fi were right behind, not far off tailgating us.

'It started when we went down to their holiday cottage in Cornwall. Simon's dad was back in Hampshire and was going to be joining us a few days later. So it was just the three of us. Simon, me and her. Anyway, one afternoon I went off for a wander on my own along the coastal path and when I got back she told me Simon had gone into the village to pick up some bread and things. So I went out into the garden and started reading a book and she came out and sat down next to me and then started asking me stuff, like what I thought of her.'

'Really?!'

'Yeah. And before I knew it, she had her hand up under my shirt and was undoing the buttons on hers and it just went from there, I suppose.'

'Bloody hell!' It was awful, dark and dangerous, but I couldn't help but admire him. 'That's incredible.'

He stubbed his cigarette out in the full ashtray. 'Yeah, I

know.' He seemed far less impressed by his own feat than I did. 'It just happened really.'

'So how long did it go on for?'

'A year and a half or so. She kept it going. Used to come up on long weekends, take me out, stuff like that.'

'So that's where you used to go. We all thought you had a girlfriend in Brighton or somewhere.'

He ran his hands through his hair. 'We often stayed there. In a hotel, on the front. She even took me abroad a few times. Stayed in some real nice hotels in Paris, Amsterdam, places like that. Got to see quite a bit of Europe.' He paused for a second. 'And a fair few hotel ceilings.'

I laughed. 'So how did it all end then?'

'I got cold feet. I mean, she was real keen. Bought me this.' Billy showed me his Omega watch.

'Amazing,' I said, referring to both the story and the watch. 'She must have really liked you.'

'Yeah, she did.'

'So how did you meet her without anyone finding out?'

'I'd walk off down the drive and meet her at the bottom. She always wore shades, even midwinter.'

'That was a bit risky, wasn't it? The bottom of the drive.'

'I think she liked taking risks.'

I doubted it was because she liked taking risks, more that Billy had an ability to get women to behave in risky ways. Like they had no control over what they were doing.

'She even got a bit frisky in the car a few times. One time, what's his name? The skinny history teacher. Used to teach Fives as well.'

'Mr Higgs?'

'Yeah, Mr Higgs. Well, he passed us on his bike while she was... you know, out of sight and... getting busy. I sat there, tried smiling and waved. Idiot just waved back.'

'You're joking!' I couldn't help but laugh at the thought of Mr Higgs cycling by as Billy was being blown off by Simon's mum and them just waving at each other.

'No. Never did it at the bottom of the drive after that.'

'I bet you didn't!'

I braked, then turned sharp left, as we crossed a narrow, stone bridge to the other side of the gorge. They were still right on our tail.

'She came over to the States to see me after I left. Couldn't put her off. It was like age was making her blind, not wise. Towards the end, she started acting like an obsessed teenager.'

'In what way?' I asked.

'Let's just say her underwear became quite a lot more provocative and... colourful.' He smiled, shook his head, let slip. 'Even leopardskin stuff.'

Increasingly, he said, there were brief but clear moments when her eyes searched anxiously for confirmation that she still had what it took to turn him on. And he believed the lingerie collection to be a part of that. Her trip to the States was as memorable for her array of underwear, he said, as it was for the variety of neon they fucked under. Motel to motel, blue, red, green flashing neon. Her plans sounded as though they were becoming wilder.

'She even talked about divorcing Simon's dad and moving out to San Francisco.'

'Shit! That really is serious.'

'I know. I think what it was, she felt kind of trapped, and bored. She once told me her husband was already talking about a place in the sun, in Portugal or somewhere, with a golf course nearby. I guess she was fighting against getting old. One last throw of the dice.'

I looked in the mirror again. They were still right behind. 'Does Simon know about it?' I asked.

'I'm not sure. His dad found out about it though.'

'Oh dear. How was that?'

'I wrote her a letter. I should have fucking phoned her. Nothing cute, just businesslike, telling her I didn't think it was a good idea her coming over again. Crap like that. Anyway, she didn't follow my instructions to rip it up as soon as she'd read it. And of course he found it and had it out with her. Then he wrote to my folks explaining what had gone on. I got a letter from him as well. Said that if he ever saw me again, he'd kill me. Wring my scrawny neck, he said. I believed him too, by the tone of his letter. Boy was he mad.'

'Nasty.'

'Yeah. Of course all the shit hit the fan after that. My dad went apeshit. Made me join the army, threatened to cut me out of the will, stuff like that. I tried telling him the truth of it, that she'd seduced me. But he wasn't interested.'

'Did you ever get in touch with her after that?'

'No way, man. My dad made me write to Simon's dad, apologising for everything. Then about six months later, I got a call from Simon, saying he wanted to come over for a holiday. I could tell he didn't know a thing about it. He sounded really excited, said he was going to buy a ticket that week. I never heard another word. I guess his dad must have stopped him. I've no idea what happened after that. Don't really want to ask either.'

We drove past a bunch of fresh flowers up against the rock face, commemorating the dead at the scene of a final accident.

'I wouldn't mind finding out, though,' he continued. 'Still think about it sometimes.' He paused for a moment, and stroked his jaw. 'I bet they got divorced.'

'Even if they did, you're not totally to blame if she seduced you. Anyway you were young.'

'Yeah, but I let her seduce me. As for being young, I'm not sure how much that has to do with it. I mean, I think I was old enough to know what I was doing.' He paused for a moment. 'They were good to me, Dan. Real good. And Simon was a buddy.'

On that road, after what he'd told me, I should have taken the right fork out of Panes and put them all on the first flight out of Bilbao. I just knew there was going to be trouble. There was no clear shape or detail to it. Just a vague yet certain sense that it now spread its black wings over us. But instead of trusting my instinct and acting on it, I chickened out, tried not to see it because I was so bloody obsessed with making sure everyone had a good time. It's the worst turn I've ever taken.

99

Coming through a land of orchards, we arrived in Cangas de Onís, the last town before Covadonga and the lakes. For the last two hours or so, I'd hardly noticed the apple trees, the gorge and mountains, as he told me his story. Instead I saw military planes and SCUD alerts, leopardskin underwear and neon motel signs, four-star hotel beds in Brighton and the desperate grasp of a beautiful woman, pulling the threads together.

After a quick stop to get some chorizo, bread and water, we made the final leg of the journey up to the lakes. We started to climb steep; steep enough to have to slip into first gear a few times, over the swathes of painted graffiti on the road which were there because a stage of La Vuelta a España finishes at the top. In fact, the whole country was gripped by cycling fever that month as Miguel Indurain attempted to win a fifth consecutive Tour de France. If he was a legend with four, he was to become a god after five.

We passed a group of three cyclists going up to Covadonga. They had all the gear on, lycra jerseys with sponsorship all over them, cycling shoes and caps. And they weren't messing around. Their veins were full to bursting and their skin shone with sweat.

'You're going the wrong way boys! France is that-a-way!' Billy yelled from his window.

I was pleased to see he had bucked up a bit. He was on good form, as if what he'd told me earlier had taken pounds off his shoulders. He was as lightened up as I'd seen him all trip.

'Have you ever wondered what people get out of watching cycling live?' I asked. 'I mean, you wait around for hours for them to come along and then they pass you by in a flash. I can understand why people get into it on TV. You get to see the whole race. But live?'

'You've gotta be a real cycling nut, I guess.'

'I suppose you could say the same thing about the encierros in Pamplona. You wait for ages and the bulls and runners pass you in a split second.'

'But that's got the added thrill of blood. It's like motor racing. There's no way it would be so popular if it wasn't so dangerous. There's the added excitement of a wipe-out.'

We didn't stop at the monastery in Covadonga, but carried on round the bend and up the hill. The cafés on the roadside were busy with tourists and the souvenir stalls looked to be doing a brisk trade.

We soon reached the lakes, quiet and other-worldly in contrast, just odd figures dotted about, traipsing the shore through the faint mist that hung low over the water, like fettered ghosts.

From there we climbed some more and it was a short drive along a rough stone track to the refugio, a solitary stone building on a grassy plain with a forest in the valley ahead and beyond that, the huge saw-toothed peaks that form the western massif. Wild horses grazed nearby.

'Wow! Isn't this great?! We're going to have a lot of fun in here tonight,' Fi said, as we put our bags into the small dormitory, where we appeared to be the only guests.

'I know!' Eddy said.

'Just get practising on how to run the gauntlet,' Billy said.

'I'd forgotten about that,' she said.

'No, none of that for me. I'm saving my running for Pamplona.'

I looked at Eddy, not sure if he was joking. But I did know if he was fool enough to run, the bulls would have an easy enough target to aim at.

Billy, Simon and I got changed into shorts and boots and we all went back down to the cars.

'Don't you want these, then?' Simon asked Fi, holding the bunch of flowers he'd picked up from off the back seat. The heat in the car had caused them to wilt slightly.

'Yes, I do. It just slipped my mind, that's all.'

'Do you want to give them to the warden to sort out?' he asked, handing them to her.

'Yes, of course.'

Fi went inside with the flowers and when she returned, we divided the food. Then she and Eddy drove back down to the monastery and we set off on our hike for Mirador de Ordiales.

This was a proper walk and on a clear day, like we had, it's worth getting up high for. From the Mirador, you can see mountains as far south and west as your eyes can take you, the sea to the north, and if you scramble a hundred yards or so higher over some craggy terrain, then you get to see the lakes, down towards the sea.

The afternoon sun was strong so we stopped regularly to catch our breath and drink water. We stopped for a late lunch at another refugio, Vega Redonda, an hour and a half from where we started. We were high up, at about 5,000 feet. Just the sound of wind and cow bells.

'How are your boots, Simon?' I asked.

'Fine. No hint of a blister yet.'

Billy lay back on the grass in front of the refugio, eyes shut with his head clasped in his hands. He yawned.

'Tired?' Simon asked.

'A bit.'

'What time did you get to bed?'

'Late.'

'I know it was late. What time roughly?'

'No idea.'

Billy stood up, flexed his bad leg, then walked inside the refugio.

'I'm sorry for last night,' Simon said.

'It's all right. These things happen.'

'Did you stay up with Fi and Billy?'

'No. I went before.'

'And was Billy much after you?'

'I don't know. I was asleep by the time he got in.' I realised as soon as I said it, I should have lied. I should have told him Billy was in straight after me. Instead my comments must have fed his worry. 'Mind you I was asleep as soon as my head hit the pillow,' I added.

Simon nodded, nibbling at the skin around his fingers as he looked out across the mountains.

After some bread and wild boar chorizo we climbed some more, along the narrow winding path, which in winter is hidden by snow. It's dangerous up here in the winter. A couple of years ago a German student fell through a canopy of snow and into a deep gulley. They found his bones the following spring.

I think being so high up bonded us. It was like old schooldays again, the three of us relaxed and together. And it was an experience we'd always share, no matter what. When we reached Mirador de Ordiales we sat down and took it all in, the fresh air and stunning views, views that seemed to stretch all the way to America, over the top of uncountable golden peaks. It wasn't a time for talking.

To the east, about sixty yards away, a chamois skipped across the mountainside, breaking the silence with the occasional slide of scree, as clear on the ear as though it were only a few feet away.

Billy stood up and looked out west again and then over the edge, where the mountain vanishes and several hundred feet of sheer drop appears. 'Wow!' he said.

Simon and I stood up and peered over the wall of rock that Billy was looking over. Birds glided on the wind, hundreds of feet below us. Even though the wall of rock protected us from falling and made it safe, I couldn't help but lose my stomach from imagining the fall as I threw myself to the lush matchbox fields below.

I put my fleece on as it was windy up there, and now we weren't moving, it was getting a fair bit colder as well. Simon peeled an orange, which he shared. And Billy lit a spliff he'd rolled earlier in the car. He pulled on it a few times and then passed it to Simon.

'Thanks, Billy. This really will put us up in the land of the gods.' He took a few sharp drags on it, then inspected

Billy's construction. 'You know, I haven't done this in a while. A long while.' He pulled on it deeply, then passed it to me. 'Do you still do a lot of drugs then, Billy?' he asked.

'No, not really.'

'Any acid?'

'No way. Those days are over.'

'So you finally conquered the demons within then?' he asked.

Billy picked up a jagged piece of stone and skimmed it over the edge. 'Maybe I didn't find as many as I thought I would in the first place.' He paused for a moment, then added, 'That was then though.'

It had been Billy's thing at school. He'd had a bad trip once and so he decided to go back and keep taking the stuff until he exorcised what he called 'the demons in his head'.

'Well, you're a braver man than me, Billy.'

'And me as well,' I said.

'I don't know about that. I suppose I just wasn't very frightened of that much. When I was younger it just never occurred to me. That's why I'd do a lot of risky shit, regardless of what might happen. I was blind to the consequences. But one or two things happened that made me think. And now I have to face up to them.'

Simon looked down at his new boots and dislodged a stone from the sole. 'Yes,' he said. 'I suppose we all do.'

'I suppose I'm just more aware of how precious life is.'

A minute later, Billy climbed up onto the rock and crawled to the edge, the dangerous bastard.

Simon was still looking down at his new boots, with his head in his hands now.

'Are you all right?' I asked.

'Yes… Yes, I'm fine.'

'God, what a way to go!' Billy shouted.

'Is it?' Simon asked, frowning. He took a deep breath through his nostrils.

Then he climbed up and inched his way towards the soles of Billy's boots. He crept up alongside him and they both looked down to the drop below. I could hear them talking but couldn't make out what they were saying, as the wind blew their words apart, sent syllables high and wide.

What Billy did next was to stun me, shock me to the point where I didn't believe it was really happening. He stood up and stepped back, watching his feet as he moved towards the edge.

'Billy!' I shouted. 'Get away from there!'

'This is my holiday. I'm having some fun now!' he shouted back.

And back he went until the heels of his boots were over the edge. He rocked up and down on his toes. 'So, I like it dangerous, do I?! How out of control am I now, then?!' he yelled at Simon.

I remember the sound of it more than anything. It was like the crackle of a badly scratched record as the rock beneath his feet snapped and crumbled. I can't really picture him falling. All I remember is Simon standing up as I climbed up onto the plateau and scrambled on all fours towards them. And I clearly remember seeing Billy's fingers

clawing and straining with all they had, and Simon just
standing there looking down at him. I'll never forget that.
The way he looked down at him like an indifferent
observer. I peered over the edge, saw Billy frantically trying
to find a foothold that wasn't there. I reached down,
grabbed his forearm with both hands.

'Well help me, will you?' I shouted. 'For fuck's sake!'

Simon seemed to snap out of it, then grabbed his other
forearm and we yanked with all we had. We tried pulling
him up, but our hands slipped slowly, torturously slowly,
up his sun-creamed forearms. I caught a glimpse of him
looking up at us, eyes so alive with fast thought and fear.
We pulled with all we had, but still he slipped. Billy wasn't
looking at us any more, but down to his feet, and possibly
beyond, to the huge drop below. My hands clung to his
wrist, and then to the top of his hand. I was looking up at
the sky, straining so hard I thought my temples would
explode, when he finally broke away. There was no last
scream or yell from the depths of his stomach. Just silence.
I looked down, sickened to the core. Then my stomach
relaxed. He'd hardly moved at all. He'd managed to find a
foothold, then a place to secure himself with his hands and
he clambered to safety. He lay out on his back panting hard,
clutching his bad leg again.

'What the fuck were you playing at, Billy?!' I asked, also
breathing hard, bent close to double. 'You're a dangerous,
crazy bastard. You know that?'

'Yeah,' he said, still panting and looking skyward. 'I know
that.'

The light was starting to fade as we came back down, but it was a route I was familiar with. I'd come down in moonlight before. I still couldn't believe what Billy had done. He almost died up there, it was absolutely crazy, and I was certain it was to do with what they'd talked about on the edge, what I couldn't hear. I was pretty sure the smoke had brought it on, especially so high up. Definitely for Simon; he wasn't used to smoking these days. And it had all seemed fine between them earlier on, as if they'd settled their differences. Then how quickly it changed.

It was a beautiful sunset, and I forgot about earlier for moments, minutes, even quarters of hours. Shades of purple slipped through valleys, reds and oranges glanced over mountain tops, and glittering silvers tickled the ocean. The sky was cloudless. I remember thinking we were going to see a lot of stars that night.

'Did you have a nice walk?' Fi asked. She was sitting cross-legged, Buddha-like, on the grass meadow in front of the refugio with Eddy.

'Yes,' Simon said. 'Quite adventurous.' He looked across at Billy, then bent down and kissed Fi on the lips.

'Are you not cold?' I asked Eddy. He was lying down on his side. Shirt off, he resembled a seal resting on a beach.

'I should put my top on really. It is starting to get a bit cold.' He reached to his side and put a short-sleeved shirt on.

'Well we've been getting religious,' Fi said.

'How was it?' I asked.

'Great. Very busy though.'

'We've been getting religious too. And high with it,' Simon said.

'I thought you all looked a bit stoned. Well, thanks for inviting us for a smoke,' Fi said.

'Don't worry. I've got plenty more,' I said.

It surprised me that Fi was a smoker. She just didn't look the sort.

We eased our boots off on the steps of the refugio and then went inside to the lounge area and sat at the wooden table to the right of the empty fireplace. The bunch of flowers that Simon had bought Fi were on the table, in a jug.

Within the hour we were tucking into a big meal of pork fillets and chips, washed down with a few bottles of rosé. There was nothing else left on the menu, just pork and chips. It didn't matter though. It was wholesome food, and Eddy approved. And even if he hadn't, it wouldn't have mattered. All food tastes good in the mountains and opinions on culinary matters carry far less weight when you're high up and everything's so basic. Mountains are great for making you appreciate what you have.

'Billy and I were talking earlier on the way up about wipe-outs,' I said.

'Yeah.' He chewed on his fillet, sliced another piece off, didn't add any more.

I carried on. 'It does draw people in, doesn't it?'

'Skiing's my favourite for wipe-outs,' Eddy said.

'You can't beat a good motorbike pile-up in my opinion,'

Simon reckoned. 'Though you're right, skiing's pretty decent as well.'

'And bullfighting,' Eddy said. 'I was looking through a Spanish newspaper a couple of days ago and there was this amazing photo of a bullfighter in mid-air.'

'Blood and gore. We lap it up, all of us,' Simon said. 'It's what sells papers.'

It was my turn again. My turn to take the baton and run the distance. 'That's right. It was like the time last year in Santander when this pack of stray dogs attacked an old man on the beach. As it happened, some guy walking by just above the beach had a camera and shot the whole lot of it. And then he sold his film to the newspaper. Didn't drop his camera to help the poor old sod out. Oh no, he just kept shooting off the film. Sold a lot of copies though.'

'Bloody coward,' Fi said. 'That's disgusting.'

I didn't point out that I wouldn't have dived in there either. I'm not brave or crazy enough for that sort of thing. They'd have probably set on me. But I wouldn't have snapped away in cold blood. I would have phoned an ambulance or something, at least.

'What happened to him?' Fi asked.

'He managed to get away. Swam out to sea.'

'Lucky he could swim,' Eddy said.

'Raises an interesting point, about a photographer's responsibilities,' Billy said, finally joining in. 'I mean, take war photographers, for example. Like Robert Capa. He was meant to have charted new territory as a war photographer. But what about all those guys that followed in his footsteps?'

There was a moment's silence before finally Simon spoke, like none of us knew what he meant. 'What about them?'

'Well, what I'm saying is, are we not saturated with enough war photos by now?'

'Yes. And?... And so what?' Simon asked.

'Well, I think there's quite a strong case that once they've shot enough film, they could put their cameras down and actually help out.'

'Wouldn't that compromise their impartiality though?'

Billy sipped on his wine before answering Simon. 'Yeah, but come on. You're smart enough not to believe all that crap. I mean no one, not even photographers or reporters, can ever be impartial, let alone when it's really going off, when they're right in the thick of it.'

'No, you're right. But they still have to try and maintain that credibility, if only for pretence's sake. And anyway, look at it on the cynical side. Business operates and business rules, and it's the best shots that sell. Business is dictated by cut-throat reality and unfortunately our little protests would never be able to change it, however much we tried.'

'But you've gotta keep trying though.'

'But why?' Simon asked him. 'If there's nothing you can do?'

Billy looked over to the empty fireplace. 'Because it's better to keep a clean slate, I suppose.'

'Signs of a conscience emerging? Not like the Billy of old.' Billy didn't reply. He looked at Simon before inspecting his clean plate. Fi fidgeted on the bench. Simon carried on. 'OK, so let's take this scenario, then. Imagine you're on a ship and it's sinking. And imagine there's nothing you can do about it. It's going down whatever and there's no way off. However fast you bail out the water with the buckets, it's going down. Now what do you do? Do you keep bailing out the water in the engine room and, as you say, keep trying? Or do you sit in the bar with your drink and go down smiling?'

'And there's no way off?'

Simon sat back and put his hands behind his head. 'No.'

'I don't know. I've never really thought about it.'

'I know what I'd do,' I said. 'I'd stay in the bar and drink.'

'My point exactly,' Simon said.

'Pretty pessimistic view though that there's no way out,' Billy pointed out.

'But given the scenario, it's an obvious decision,' Eddy said. He held his glass up and looked into it before taking a drink.

'I don't know if it is though,' Fi said. 'I can see both points of view. The bar's for a certain lot. Pleasure seekers, possibly cowards. But that's not the whole world. I mean there are other raisons d'être. And anyway, I don't think it's a very good scenario. Human nature would never accept such an inevitability. People would naturally struggle to get off even if it was impossible.'

'I'm sure they would. But it was just a hypothetical situation, darling. And nothing more than that.'

That night we all got stoned in the refugio after dinner and we smoked with the warden, who joined us after I told him how much we'd enjoyed the meal and after he'd washed up. He looked at the end of his forties, but his manner was younger. His well-rounded stomach suggested comfortable living and, at a guess, it was probably a life outdoors that had etched the lines and grooves on his face.

We were the only guests there that night, surprising given that it was summer. Still, it was midweek I suppose. The warden looked happy to have a quiet night of it. At one point he got up and came back from the kitchen with a bottle of orujo and six glasses.

'Oh no, here we go!' Eddy said.

The warden looked at Eddy and smiled, then poured out six glasses. He picked his up and held it in front of him. 'Salud,' he said.

'Salud,' I replied.

We all clinked glasses and drank.

The warden asked me what we all did and I explained in Spanish. He was curious about Simon. 'Anuncios,' he said. He looked at him for a moment, nodding and rubbing his chin before his eyes narrowed. 'Anuncios. Debe ser un trabajo muy interesante, no?' he asked, all the while looking at Simon.

'What's he saying?' Simon asked me.

'He was saying advertising must be interesting.'

'Yes, it is.'

The warden asked me what advert he was working on at the moment. I told him Simon was doing an advert for an oil company.

The warden nodded and topped up the glasses with more orujo.

Billy covered the glass with his hand. 'No, gracias,' he said.

'Joder! Venga tío.'

'Go on,' I said. 'It'd be rude not to really.'

Billy took his hand off the glass and smiled at the warden. The warden slapped Billy on the back and topped him up.

'I was thinking earlier as we were walking that this would be a great place to shoot the advert. The company wants to present an environmentally friendly image and you've got the lot here. Mountains, wildlife. It'd be ideal really. I might even suggest it when I get back.'

'Qué dice?'

'Que este lugar sería un buen lugar para rodar un anuncio,' I explained to the warden.

He scratched his head like there were fleas in amongst his thick grey hair and turned round to look at the empty fireplace.

Billy sipped on his orujo and then twisted his glass round slowly on the table. He didn't look at Simon, just at the table and what he was doing. 'You are joking, aren't you?'

'No. Why should I be?'

He looked up at Simon and smiled. 'The wind-up merchant, par excellence.'

Simon looked back at Billy with his fingers linked and the tips of his thumbs resting on his chin. 'Not at all. It's totally in keeping with the image they're trying to create.'

Billy started laughing and shaking his head. 'No way, man!'

'Seriously.'

He looked hard at Simon, smiles all gone. 'And you're quite happy to help a bunch of murdering fucking crooks make a fortune by promoting an image that's a lie, just so that you can make a few bucks out of it?'

'I wouldn't mind a buck right now,' Eddy said.

His attempt at a joke fell flat.

'It's called business, Billy. It's the way the bloody world works. I don't like it either, but there's nothing I can do that can change it. And if I didn't do it, someone else would. There are hundreds of people queuing up for my job. Hundreds.'

'So you're just going to go along with an industry that's fucked Africa over, raped the fucking place, raped wherever it can get its filthy paws on? You know, you might have made a fortune, but you've lost all your ideals somewhere along the way.'

'And since when have you been so bloody moral yourself then, Billy?' Simon snapped.

'Simon, please. Not now,' Fi said. She looked nervous as she put her hand on his knee and started rubbing it. 'Come on. Just leave it.'

'It's a perfectly reasonable question,' he said, eyes fixed on Billy. 'I just wanted to hear his answer, that's all, given that morals are such a... "familiar" subject to you, wouldn't you say?'

Billy's nostrils started to flare. 'What are you getting at?'

'Nothing.'

'I wish you'd just spit it out!'

'Well, you brought up the question of morality, mate. Since when have you been such a global crusader then?'

'I'm not a global crusader.' Billy knocked back his orujo and slammed the glass on the table. 'I'm just anti-petrol companies and any bastard that helps them on their way.'

'Are you calling me a bastard?' Billy didn't reply. 'And as if you haven't supported them. How the hell do you think we'd have got up here without a car? By camel? Magic carpet, perhaps? Join the real world, will you?'

'Don't get funny with me, Simon. It's easy enough for you to talk about it from your office desk and your padded seat, but I fought in a war over petrol.'

'I think you'll find the Gulf war was a bit more complicated than that, mate.'

'Oh right, so you were out there, were you? You know just what it was like, what it was all about? You know what it was like to get shot at, do you?'

'No, I don't. But I do know about shooting, Billy.'

'Look, just shut up, the pair of you!' Fi interrupted. 'For God's sake!'

'Yes, come on,' I said.

But Billy didn't pay us any attention. 'And what the fuck would you know about it?'

Simon leant forward, his elbows resting on the table. His eyes went right into Billy. And then those haunting words. 'I know a lot about shooting, Billy. A lot.'

Billy got up and grabbed his glass, drew it behind his shoulder, aimed at Simon. Then he turned away, looked back at him, shaking his head, turned away again, and hurled it as hard as he could into the fireplace. Thick glass fractured against sooted stone and he left the room and went outside, slamming the front door behind him. He was as angry as I'd ever seen him.

Fi stood up instinctively.

'Don't!' Simon said. His voice softened, implored. 'Please don't.'

She dropped her head, placed her hands on the table, lowered herself slowly back into the chair.

'I better go out and see how he is,' I said.

It took me a few moments to spot him beyond the light coming from the refugio window. The joint tip glowed orange, died down, burned strong and bright again in pitch black, like a lighthouse warning ships away from the rocks. I walked over, sat on the same rock, cold now that the sun had left it, listened to the cow bells gently chime.

'Are you all right?' I asked.

'Yeah.' He dragged on the spliff again before passing it to me. He leant forward and put his head in his hands. 'I don't know. I just think what he does is the pits.'

'I know, but try not to fall out about it. I mean, we're all going to have different opinions on some things, aren't we?'

'Yeah, but what's the point being all sweet with someone just for the sake of it? It stinks.'

'OK. So maybe what he wants to do stinks. But he doesn't stink.'

Billy looked across at me. 'What you do defines you.'

'Only for eight hours a day,' I pointed out. 'Not the whole day.'

What I didn't point out though, was that if he was right about what he'd just said – that what you do defines you –

then what you have done to you also defines you, like having a close friend sleep with your mother, for example. Somehow I don't think he'd have appreciated that.

'Maybe.' He didn't sound convinced.

Maybe it was the spliff or the orujo, or being reminded of the war, but the way Billy was now talking about Simon was pretty well a pole apart from what he'd said just a few hours earlier, with what had seemed like something approaching remorse as well, about how he'd ruined their friendship. And now here he was, spitting real venom at the same person, as if Simon was someone else. And Simon probably was, after what had happened.

We smoked the rest of the spliff in silence.

'Come on. Shall we go back in? Let's just try and forget about it, shall we?' I said, as Billy squashed the roach into the rock.

He looked up at the stars. 'You know, there's something I haven't told you, Dan.'

'What?'

He ran his hand, fast, backwards and forwards over thinning hair. 'I killed a boy in the Gulf.'

I didn't reply. I didn't know what to say.

'He was just a kid. Couldn't have been more than thirteen. I had to see him. They told me not to. Never look into the eyes of someone you've killed, they said. But I had to. The open mouth, the eyes staring straight ahead. He was no longer the enemy. He was just a poor kid, probably from some poor family whose lives would never be the same again because their son had gotten on the wrong end of my bullet. And later on, I got hit in the thigh and was flown back to the States and spent some time in hospital. I wrote a letter to his family to say I was sorry but there was no way of finding out who he was so I never sent it. And besides, I don't think he'd have had any qualms if it had been the other way round. He'd have shot me like a dog, I'm sure. No, I wasn't sorry for what I'd done. More for the consequences of those left behind.'

'And you left the army soon after?'

'Yeah.'

'What did you do?'

'Drank too much.'

'Was that to do with the boy?'

'No.' He paused for a moment. 'Maybe. I don't know. It's weird, you know, you take away something as structured as the army, and you're left with nothing, even though you hate what you've left.' He shook his head and smiled. 'What the hell? Come on. Let's go back in.'

We walked back into the room, eight anxious eyes on us.

'I'm sorry, Simon,' Billy said.

Simon stood up. 'I'm sorry, too,' he said and hugged him. He looked sorry for what had happened. And he looked eager for peace.

'Pues voy a coger otra botella de orujo,' the warden said. He looked happy with the reconciliation as well and rubbed his hands before leaving the room to get another bottle of orujo, and a new glass for Billy.

And Eddy cracked a couple of jokes. They weren't that

funny really if I remember rightly, but we laughed hard, much more than we'd probably have done if there hadn't been that scene. The warden came back not only with orujo but also with a pack of cards. He showed us a game and we played for an hour or so. Simon won.

By the end of the game, you'd never have guessed there'd been an argument earlier. And at one o'clock we went upstairs to the dormitory. I set the alarm clock for half six as we had a long drive to Pamplona. Then Eddy turned the lights out. There were to be no pillow fights that night and no one ran the gauntlet.

PAMPLONA

The warden was in the kitchen, sharpening long knives, as we said goodbye. I apologised for the argument the night before.

'No pasa nada, tío. Oye. Ten cuidado con los toros,' he said. He put the knife down on the wooden chopping board and shook my hand with a firm look in his eye. Although I'm sure he didn't mean to, he almost crushed my bones.

'What did he say?' Billy asked.

'Be careful of the bulls,' I said. I spread my fingers out wide, low down and out of sight, like they were a duck's webbed feet.

'Sí,' Billy said to him. 'Muchas gracias.'

We stepped outside and walked to the cars. Billy's leg had got worse again, no doubt due to his fall at the top of the mountain.

Eddy rubbed his hands briskly. 'I think the bulls will have to be careful of me,' he said.

I looked at him and smiled. It was hard to tell from his expression if he was serious about running or not. And then just for a moment as I scanned his ruddy face, I saw matted blood in flaxen hair – his blood, his hair – and more of his blood mixed with his tears slipping down past his ears as he lay on the cobbled street and said his last dying bloody words to me. 'Dan, I told you. I think the bulls will have to be careful of me!' I wasn't going to let him run. After all, we were family now, both uncles, connected on different sides to the same new, tiny piece of the jigsaw, created by the mixture of his sister's blood with my brother's. And how I hated being connected just then.

Eddy walked over to our car, like he wanted to come with us, but Simon asked him if he'd give him a hand reading the map, in case we ended up getting separated.

Fi shook her head. 'He doesn't think I'm up to it,' she said.

'I do. It's just to be on the safe side. We don't want a repeat of France last year, do we?'

'Look, if we do get separated, we'll meet you in Pamplona at the nearest café to the right of the Hotel La Perla in the main square.'

'What's it called again?' Fi asked me. She dug into her handbag and pulled out a pen and a scrap of paper.

'La Perla. P. E. R. L. A.,' I said, as she wrote it down on the paper, on the bonnet of Simon's car. 'Hemingway slept there,' I added.

'Will we be able to get rooms there?' she asked. She tucked the piece of paper back into her handbag.

'No way. The whole town will be jam-packed. You have to reserve somewhere months in advance. You might as well leave your bags in the car. We're going to be up all night anyway.'

'Great!' she said, without a hint of irony.

Once I had negotiated the tricky mountain roads and we

were on straighter, more open highway, I decided to ask him. 'What were you and Simon talking about yesterday?'

'When?'

'Before you almost... almost killed yourself.'

'Nothing much.'

'Right. So why did you shout something at him about being out of control?'

'I don't know really.'

'Billy, I wish you'd be fucking straight with me for a change. You owe me that much now, at least.'

'I didn't ask for your help,' he said. He took one of my cigarettes and lit it. 'He just asked me if anything happened between me and Fi in that abandoned hut, that's all.'

'And?' I prompted.

'I told him that nothing had gone on.' He opened his window, blew smoke out. 'I don't think he believed me. Just started smiling and shaking his head. And even if anything did happen, I'd hardly have told him. Not up there. Then he started getting all cryptic on me. I don't know why he just couldn't be upfront about it.'

It crossed my mind that that was rather rich coming from Billy. 'What did he say?'

'Said I liked it dangerous, that it wouldn't be the first time I was out of control. I asked him what he meant by that, and he wouldn't tell me and so I did my little dance routine... I don't know what the hell he meant by that.'

'Is it that important to you?'

'No, of course it isn't. Well, big deal if he was referring to his mother. I don't know where he thinks I've been for

123

the last few years, but having an affair with a married woman doesn't exactly figure high on my list of life's great crimes. Besides, his parents were never that happy anyway.'

I joined him with a cigarette, and remember thinking he hadn't got it straight in his head, or at least a consistent view on the matter, about how he saw their affair and his role in it. But looking at it now, I guess he never had that luxury. No one with any brain does, I suppose, when they're in that deep.

'Let's sort everything out after the fiesta,' I said, 'and have a good time.'

He looked straight ahead. 'Stupid asshole,' he said, like he was talking to himself.

And there was no way of telling if he was referring to me or Simon, or himself, for that matter.

The roads to Pamplona took us past Bilbao again but instead of going on to San Sebastián, we turned right soon after Bilbao and took the road to Vitoria. It's a sharp climb to start with along winding wooded roads, but once on the top the tarmac levels out and stretches right out in front of you, and we were soon driving through the plains near Vitoria.

We stopped for a coffee break, on the ring road just outside of Vitoria, at a roadside café with a petrol station next to it. We needed to gas up. And I needed to stretch my legs and back.

I also needed to talk to Simon, and tell him that I believed Billy when he said nothing had happened between him and Fi – even though I wasn't sure myself. I was desperate to smooth the way for Pamplona, clear the air, so we could concentrate on enjoying the fiesta.

Even though the café was almost empty it was full of vibrant noise. The coffee machine hissed and gurgled and accompanied the electronic tunes from the fruit machine, as a round, middle-aged man filled it with coins. We drank our coffees up at the bar. Billy then went to the toilet. Eddy walked over to the window with Fi and inspected the tapes for sale.

'Simon, can I have a quick word?'

We stepped outside. A huge truck rolled by on the main road. We walked round the side of the building and sat on the low wall. In the dusty car park below, I noticed a condom and a discarded syringe. An empty Coke can rattled thinly as the wind pushed it towards a parked car.

'I suppose you want to talk about Billy, don't you?'

'Yes.'

'Well let's get one thing straight before we start. I came out here in good faith, Dan. There's something I need to sort out with him, but I never came out here looking for trouble.'

It was as close as he'd come to telling me he knew about Billy's affair with his mother. 'I know that,' I said.

'He's pushing me to the limit, Dan, messing around with Fi, and slagging off what I do for a living. He even mocks my religious beliefs. It's like he wants to annihilate me. I'm trying my best to keep a lid on it, but he's not making it easy for me. And last night, I almost let him have it. I was that close.' With his index finger and thumb almost touching, he demonstrated how close.

'I think you should take Billy's word for it, you know? He swore to me, on his mother's life, that nothing happened with him and Fi,' I lied.

'On his mother's life,' he repeated, as if repeating the words helped him digest them. 'You know, I'm not sure what to believe any more.'

I looked down at the condom and syringe again. 'Look, just trust him. And let's just enjoy the fiesta.'

Back on that long straight road again, driving across the parched plains, Billy asked me, 'What were you talking about with Simon back there at the gas station?'

'Nothing much.'

'Don't start that with me.'

'Oh, as if you haven't done it yourself. OK, so if you want to know, I told him to trust you.'

'You didn't mention anything about me and his mother, did you?'

I swerved to avoid what turned out to be a squashed cat in the road. I looked in the mirror and saw Simon do the same. 'God, Billy, what do you take me for? Of course I fucking didn't. I want this whole thing buried and forgotten about. Not dragged with us through the streets of Pamplona. This is your mess, Billy, and I wish you'd have the fucking decency to keep it that way.'

'So you don't think he knows then?'

'No,' I lied, once more that day. 'Not a bloody thing.'

From the by-pass round Vitoria the road runs straight through to Pamplona, much of it enclosed by hills either side but far enough away to give you a sense of space. Coming through the hills and onto more open terrain we could see Pamplona. The hay in the fields lay in circular bales, neatly wrapped like giant Swiss rolls. To the right Billy spotted a scrap yard, cars piled high on top of each other, like corpses waiting to be buried in a mass grave. A plane winged its way into Pamplona airport. I was starting to get excited, and all that had gone on before between Simon and Billy began to shrink in my mind as the thrill of fiesta took over. I was looking forward to this.

I had never been to San Fermín, but I felt as though I had. I'd seen the encierro on TV countless times – a choppy sea of red and white runners in a narrow street sliced down the middle by a charging black and brown huddle. Amongst the bulls are steers to guide them from the corral to the ring. They're calmer than the bulls because they've been castrated, and they help to keep them in a herd. My friend José had explained it to me. Back in the days when there weren't any trucks to take them to the ring – only drovers – the idea was to get the six bulls out of the corral and into the pens under the stands of the bullring where they'd later be let out to meet a matador and their death in the afternoon. Then some maniacs decided it would be a good idea to run along in front. And later on the trucks came, the drovers went, but the custom stayed.

I'd also learned that most of the trouble at the encierros usually occurs with the loose bulls, ones that have been separated from the herd. And with nearly two thousand people a day now running at San Fermín, if somebody falls, it's like a domino effect and it's not hard to imagine what a loose bull can do in that situation.

I'd heard the tales of wild drinking, of young men up all night, of Americans, Brits, Aussies and Japanese taking on the bulls for a dare, for a laugh. And I'd heard the stories of foreigners just about able to stand, attempting to run for their lives.

I have it on good authority that Hemingway never actually ran. Back in his day only the Spaniards ran. The ex-pat crowd was there to watch, to be entertained, as the drinking classes were accustomed. Entertained by theatre of the most elemental: visceral, knife-edged drama where no one knew – and no one could know – the end of the play. But even now, with the fiesta's international appeal, I don't think he'd have run. He'd have been too well informed for that; he knew too much about bulls. He was more than aware of their huge power and magnificence and the damage they could do and I reckon he'd have been humble and sensible enough, and honest enough with himself, to leave it to the experts. He realised they were to be treated with the awed respect they deserved. No, he was too clued up on bulls to take them lightly. And I reckon he'd have viewed all the pissed-up, flippant foreigners that now run as disrespectful and idiotic and would have turned his back on Pamplona. That's the irony of it. Through his book *Fiesta*, he has helped turn San Fermín into a fiesta he'd probably have avoided like the plague.

Besides he was probably in no state at seven in the morning to do anything other than watch it from a hotel window, from the comfort of a balcony with a glass of pernod in hand, like his hero Jake Barnes in *Fiesta*. Jake was Hemingway really though, wasn't he? His idealised self. A friend of mine who studied American Literature told me that in the first draft of *Fiesta*, Jake was actually called Hem. Then later on, he changed the name to Jake. And the story's so close to a real-life adventure of his, travelling down to Pamplona from Paris with a group of ex-pats, that it's hard to imagine Jake being anyone other than Hemingway.

Amazing memories, him and Jake, considering how much they drank. And they both seemed to find some sort of heroic stoicism in a bottle. Just like me... in my dreams. Me, the cool, hard-drinking man's and woman's man. The complete Renaissance man, only I wasn't much good on a horse. I could learn though. I could learn. Yeah, dream on, Danny. Dream on.

How I'd love to see that hide of myth skinned from his back. See him weeping and exposed, if only for a moment, because a generation of men – men from my father's time – have held him, and others like him, as an idol to shine a light on the way men should act, should be. Real men. Like I do as well, at times, because I can't escape my father. I'd like to think I'm not stupid or unreasonable enough though, to place all the blame at Hemingway's feet. But he's a factor all right. And I resent him for it. Because I've never even come close to having an emotionally sensitive conversation with my dad; not once has he let himself go

129

enough to cry in front of me – sin of sins – even though on several occasions I've seen he's really wanted to. 'Fine', he'd reply, when I'd ask him if he was all right, 'I've just got something in my eye, that's all.' And it's stopped us getting through to each other, touching tender, painful places that would have given our relationship so much more. Real men don't cry or show their feelings though, do they? Well, bollocks to that. And I knew all this before Pamplona. Way before replying to his invite.

But I was still looking forward to it. The fiesta, the buzz, the morbid anticipation of danger; of possible death. Yes, a dark part of me down there somewhere was turned on by it, eager to bury and blood my nose in all the gory details. I know what it's like, you see. I once saw a man dead on the pavement in London, hit by a passing car as he stepped into the Holloway Road and I felt so alive with adrenalin when I saw him, there so soon after it had happened, sharing unsaid life lust with all the other vultures like me who were stood round watching as the paramedics tried and failed to save him, feasting on the morbid details of his miserable death. I'm not proud of it but that was how I felt. I'm sorry. Sorry for all those people who have been left behind to pick up the pieces and rebuild their ruined lives.

The first we saw of it was on the outskirts of town, the odd figure in a white shirt, white trousers and white shoes with a red sash tied round the waist and a red handkerchief round the neck. There were so few people as we approached the old city walls that I began to think we might have missed it, that it was all over, that I'd got my dates wrong. It was only as we drove under the high arch in the city walls and into the centre that we caught the periphery of the fiesta. Street vendors selling red handkerchiefs, Basque berets and white T-shirts. To our left was the casco viejo and its streets were closed to traffic.

Daubed on walls left and right was ETA graffiti. It surprised me. Enara would later tell me that Navarra, with its capital Pamplona, is considered the centre of the Basque nation even though it's not a part of the officially designated 'País Vasco'.

We parked in the big central car park, just outside the casco viejo, next to the market. The majority of stalls were run by African traders, selling wooden carvings and leather goods and counterfeit watches and hippy clothes. As we walked through the market on our way to the bullring and the casco viejo, most of the traders were under plastic awnings, sitting or lying down, out of the oppressive afternoon sun. The wind had got up. It was a 'viento sur', a south wind, the worst kind, bringing nothing but dust and warm air. The wind which was said to drive people crazy. A cause of violent, erratic behaviour.

Fi stopped to try on a wide-brim straw hat. It looked good on her. Everything looked good on her; she had style, and I think she knew it. She looked at herself in the full-length mirror hanging on the side of the stall and moved the hat around a bit, then tilted it down on one side and then the other.

'What do you think?' she asked, and it was hard to tell who the question was aimed at, as she looked at us through the mirror.

'Very nice,' Simon said.

'Yeah, it suits you,' Billy added.

She smiled at herself, moving it one last time. 'I think I'll take it.'

Fi drove a hard bargain and pulled 1,000 pesetas from her purse to pay the young African trader.

'Very good, very cheap,' he said.

'Gracias,' she replied, with a smile.

He smiled back, showing off vibrant gums and a chipped front tooth. 'Que lo pases bien,' he said.

We reached the bullring. In front of us, where the street Estafeta begins, a white and red mass of people were drinking and singing and laughing, swaying, rising and dropping like a choppy sea. The cobbled streets were strewn with used plastic cups and cigarette ends and there were a few purple patches from the odd spillage, trodden-on relics of the day's debauchery so far. There wasn't long to go before the corrida and the touts were hanging around under the trees to sell their tickets; serious and alert faces that weren't a part of the revelry in front of them.

'I feel a bit left out. Shall we get a red handkerchief?' Eddy asked, as we passed a stall selling the gear. 'Join in a bit.'

'Good idea,' Billy said.

'I saw some really nice ones in the shop we passed back there,' Fi said, turning round, gesturing with her head.

'These are all right,' Eddy said. 'Three hundred pesetas. Very good. Very cheap.'

He picked one up, smelt it and felt the shiny fabric. It had a small black and white print on the back of the bulls running and underneath it said, 'San Fermín'. Pretty tacky but perfectly wearable. Besides we'd only be needing them for the night, possibly two, and they were bound to get messed up with wine stains or something.

'They'll do,' Billy said.

'I think I might just pop back to the shop and get the one I saw,' Fi said.

Billy, Eddy and I bought three handkerchiefs. Then we went back to the shop that Fi had seen and Fi and Simon bought the stylish scarves, pure cotton, with a small religious emblem on the back to do with Saint Fermín, no doubt, in whose honour the fiesta was supposed to be. We also bought some white T-shirts in the shop and changed into them while we were there. We now looked a part of the fiesta.

The whole length of Estafeta, the narrow cobbled street which the bulls would run down in the morning, was solid with revellers. Many of them were dancing to the numerous brass bands that played all along the street. These weren't official bands, just local clubs – peñas – that came to San Fermín to play in the streets and bars. They might not have been as polished as the official bands, the ones that played on TV, but how they blew and banged with all they had. They were the fiesta's heart and we were right inside it now, deafened and mesmerised by its pounding beat.

'This is amazing!' Fi shouted at me, as we stopped at the far end of Estafeta.

'Good, isn't it?' I shouted back.

'Anyone fancy a drink?' Eddy asked.

'Love one,' Simon told him. 'But where?'

It wasn't for the lack of bars that he asked. It was because every single bar was packed and it would have taken forever to get served.

'Why don't we get a bota, a wine skin?' I suggested.

Billy looked around, taking it all in. He looked bemused, and he smiled, like he hadn't expected anything quite as wild.

We found a shop at the bottom of Estafeta that sold wine skins, hundreds of them hanging from the ceiling like bloated bats. Round the corner in the general store, the old woman who served us filled our new bota with red wine and showed us how to use it. She was an expert; not a drop missed her lips. Then she spat the wine out in the sink behind her. Never let it remain empty for long, she said. The pez would stick together and you wouldn't be able to reopen it.

'No te preocupes,' I told her. There was no danger we'd leave it empty.

We had a lot of fun with it to start with. Our aim was bad enough to stain our new T-shirts without exception, as the jet of wine from the nozzle went everywhere except in the mouth. Eddy even managed to get some up his nose and Fi got some on her new scarf. Billy was the first to get the hang of it, starting close to his mouth as he squeezed, then pulling the bota away with steady hands before drawing it back in again. A couple of Spanish lads stopped to watch him. They were impressed and they laughed and clapped. Billy smiled back and then wiped his mouth with the back of his hand. He passed them the bota, and they drank from it, not a drop spilt. They passed it back to Billy, thanked us and wished us a good fiesta.

Almost an empty bota later a procession passed us, led by a marching band and followed by some sombre-looking men in bright uniforms on horseback. The horses were strong and highly strung, necks arched quarter circle and on a very tight rein. They stamped hooves from high on the cobbled street of Estafeta on their way towards the bullring.

By five o'clock the activity around the bullring had quickened. The corrida started in an hour and people were getting turned on to it. The touts were busy now, flogging overpriced tickets under the trees, in front of the ring.

I asked the others if they fancied going and none of them did at first. Simon didn't want to go because Fi didn't want to.

'Don't not go just because of me,' Fi told him.

'Are you sure you don't mind?'

'No, of course I don't.'

'Eddy?' Simon asked.

'Go on then.'

'What about you, Billy?'

'No, I'm all right. Some other time maybe.'

'Oh, come on,' he said.

'Yes, come on, Billy! We've got to get a feel for it, before we run in the morning.'

Billy sighed. 'OK. But I'm not doing any running tomorrow.'

'I'll have money on it you change your mind,' Eddy said.

'Well, you might as well hand it over now then.'

'No, you'll change your mind all right. Once we've got a few drinks down us.'

And I hoped that when Eddy saw the size of the bulls, he would change his mind as well.

I approached a thickset tout with pencil-grey hair and did the bargaining for them. I managed to get three Sol tickets next to each other for 7,000 pesetas each. I tried haggling but he wouldn't budge. There were no Sombra tickets left. I hoped they wouldn't suffer too much in the burning sun.

We walked around the Plaza in front of the bullring and took photos of each other standing next to Hemingway's bust. This was an old Papa, an 'old man and the sea' Papa, bearded, in a thick polo-neck jumper. He looks content on his plinth, wise above all, with lines fanning out from the sides of his eyes like a bundle of twigs from a witch's broom. Those lines, along with the ones etched across his forehead, told tales of a life spent chasing high and raw adventure, of big game in Africa, war in Italy, war and bulls in Spain and deep-sea fishing in Cuba, not to mention all the glamorous women and hard drinking, of course. A thousand and one mainly young Americans milled about with cameras, with the same idea as us.

After we'd taken photos, we stood about and watched yet another group of Americans smile for their cameras in front of the statue.

136

And as I sit here now and try to make sense of it all, it strikes me that maybe they were missing the point. Because as far as I understand it, Hemingway was looking to present things as they really happened, and how he really felt, rather than what you were meant or taught to feel. And yet, judging by the number of American college boys standing about in front of his statue, his book – i.e. someone else's experience they'd learnt about – influenced, and was inextricably linked to, how they felt about Pamplona. Not that we were any different, of course. We'd all read it as well. And so we were just as much seeing Pamplona through his *Fiesta*-tinted specs, whether we liked it or not.

Eddy looked over at the statue. 'It must be wonderful to drink as much as he did and write as brilliantly, plus get paid for it.'

'It couldn't have been that wonderful though,' Simon pointed out. 'He did top himself, after all.'

Billy looked at Simon and nodded. 'Yeah, that's right,' he said.

'Is that how he died? I never realised,' Fi said.

'Turned a gun on himself,' Simon told her.

'Oh God.' And she put her arm round his waist.

Eddy turned to look at them both before staring at his feet. 'Shall we have a wander, then?' he asked.

Homage paid, we strolled round the back of the Hemingway Plaza. Here we saw the Toreros and their team arrive in customised people-carriers. Their names were invariably painted in gold calligraphic font on the front, back and sides of the vehicle and portrait posters of Toreros in all their gear were stuck to the tinted windows. They got out to a rock-star reception from the crowd awaiting them and they rolled off slapdash scribbles on whatever was thrust before them by fans, on their way to a small arena, adjacent to the back of the ring. They were already changed and they looked sharp and majestic in their fine clothing, tense and ready for battle.

'Cor! He's nice,' Fi said of one of them.

Billy smiled at her. 'You like men in uniform, do you?'

'No,' she said. 'I love men in uniform.'

We arranged to meet them afterwards at the same gate they went in by.

'Keep her out of trouble now, won't you?' Simon said, and winked at me.

'I think she'll be the one keeping me out of trouble,' I said.

He kissed her and then went through the turnstiles with Billy and Eddy. Fi and I headed the other way, against the flow, to the main square, the Plaza del Castillo.

We sat outside one of the chic cafés, facing the big bandstand in the middle. Even though it had thinned out a bit, with people at the corrida, it was still busy.

We chatted for a while about their plans over a beer. 'So will you still live in London?'

'Yes. I'm not really much of a country girl. Besides, I get more ideas for my sculpture in the city.'

'I didn't know you did sculpture.'

'I just mess around, really.' She smiled at me and raised

her fine sandy eyebrows. If she was flirting with me, I think she felt very safe. Anyone must have felt safe to her, after Billy.

'Did you go to school in London?'

'No. A boarding school in Hampshire, in the middle of nowhere.'

'You didn't like it then?'

'No. I was bored and ended up getting kicked out.'

'What for?'

'Smoking dope.'

'Really? You'd have got on well with Billy at school,' I said, realising, as I said it, that they were getting on well enough as it was, right now, right here in Spain. 'He used to do a lot of drugs in those days.'

'So Simon told me.' She sipped on her beer, ran her fingers slowly through her hair, sweeping it back past her ear. 'Dan, I'm really sorry for what's been going on out here. It's not fair on you that you've become involved in all this.'

I played ignorant, hoping to draw more out of her, despite myself. 'What do you mean?'

'I just didn't expect it to work out like this. And it's my fault, really. He wasn't keen on coming in the first place. And I persuaded him. And now it's all getting out of control. I promise you, it wasn't meant to be like this.'

And I wish I'd had the balls to ask her to spell it out clearly.

We had another beer each and then wandered round the town at a gentle pace. We ended up in the Plaza del Castillo again and took seats at a different café. Fi looked around. 'Isn't that Billy over there?'

I looked over to where she was pointing, over by the bandstand. It was Billy all right, walking across the square.

'I think it is.' I shouted his name.

Billy turned round and came over.

'I thought you were at the bullfight,' I said.

He leant back and put his hands behind his head. 'I saw the first two bulls killed. That was enough to get the idea.'

'Didn't like it then?' I asked.

He shrugged his shoulders. 'It was OK. I guess I just wasn't in the mood for it.'

'Are Simon and Eddy still there?' Fi asked.

'Yeah. They're still there.'

Billy took a seat and I got the waiter's attention and ordered more drinks. We talked for half an hour or so, and I was having problems following the conversation. I was starting to feel very tired, and I could feel myself dozing off.

'I'm tired as well,' Fi said, smiling at me as I forced my eyes open once more. 'Shattered. And I haven't even done any driving.'

'Why don't we get a siesta in?' Billy suggested. 'Lie down on the grass over there for a bit.'

We walked over to the grass verge on the edge of the plaza. I lay down and was soon asleep. And when I woke, nearly an hour later, Billy and Fi had gone.

I waited for them for about fifteen minutes. Then I went to find them. Around the ring everything had quietened down.

They must have been onto the fifth or sixth bull by now. A couple of people went in and a handful of touts stood around talking to each other, looking more relaxed now the bulk of the day's business was done. As the bars opposite the ring were emptier, I stopped in one and had a coffee. From its open doors I could hear the intermittent gasps and volleys of applause. Those nimble-footed gladiators were obviously working their magic with cape and sword.

At about half eight there was an explosion of noise and people in the streets. The corrida had finished. The bands started up again, thumping huge drums and blowing trumpets. The whole world was dancing and it was hard work wading through all the revellers to the ring. It was also difficult not to give up and join in. It literally swept you along and was tempting to stop fighting the current and just go along with it. But I had obligations at the gate, so I ploughed my way through.

Simon and Eddy were there waiting for me.

'Where's Fi?' Simon asked, looking around anxiously.

'I'm not sure.'

'What do you mean?'

'I fell asleep and when I woke up she wasn't there.'

'Well, she does know where to meet us,' Eddy said.

'Did you see Billy? He left early.'

'No,' I said. I just hoped that when they reappeared they'd have the sense not to arrive together. 'So did you enjoy it?' I asked him, keen to change the subject. Eddy answered for him.

'Strong stuff. Never seen anything like it,' he said. He looked stretched, bloodless in the face, as though the event had drained him. 'An incredible spectacle. The bit I wasn't keen on though was when they actually killed the bull. There was one on its knees, all its strength gone, and this man with a dagger was stabbing it at the back of the neck and the bull couldn't move and he couldn't kill it. Must have stabbed it a good seven or eight times before it died.'

'And you, Simon?'

'Yes, yes, it was very good,' he answered quickly, sounding irritated, as though I'd distracted him. He glanced at his watch. 'Where on earth is she?'

And when she finally turned up, some ten minutes later, she arrived with Billy.

'Where have you two been?'

'Trying to get here. You can hardly move for people.'

'We decided not to wake you, Dan,' Billy said. 'We did come back but you'd gone.'

Simon looked sharply at me. He must have thought I was in on their secret, aiding and abetting. And I felt like a low-life accomplice just then.

'Oh, fuck it. Let's just go and get drunk, shall we?' I said.

We returned to the shop, bought another bottle of red wine and refilled the bota. Then we pushed our way down Estafeta, did a huge circle past the Baroque Ayuntamiento and through the Plaza del Castillo again and ended up by the bars at the bullring end of Estafeta. The bars were out in the open, makeshift, just for the fiesta, cordoned off from the thoroughfare by a slatted fence.

On the patio couples danced paso dobles. A group of six Spanish girls, young women really, were amongst them, with one girl in each pair dancing the male lead. They were strong and sure in their movements, twisting and turning in a ritual so proud and graceful, I couldn't keep my eyes off them.

'Isn't it wonderful?' Fi said, watching. 'Do you do any Spanish dancing?'

'No. A friend of mine tried teaching me but I kept treading on her toes.'

I wish I'd taken the trouble to learn though. I always felt so inadequate at fiestas, where the whole world knows how to dance, even the youngsters, and I'd stand there watching in the sidelines at a loss to know what to do with myself, before ending up at the bar.

'It's so beautiful. And it makes me really jealous. Look at Simon and Eddy. They're hypnotised.' She prodded Eddy in the ribs. 'You'll go blind, you know, if you keep staring like that.'

'I don't mind. Worth going blind for,' he said, still staring at the girls.

Two repulsively wholesome American boys – wholesome smiles, wholesome teeth and eyes, haloed with wholesome haircuts – stepped up towards the Spanish girls and tried to imitate their moves, sincerely.

Fi laughed, then clapped. 'Well, good on those boys for giving it a go.'

I looked over at Billy. He was leaning back against the fence, no expression on his face and eyes slightly glazed, as if there was no one at home.

'Are you still with us, Billy?' I asked.

'Yeah. Give us the bota, will you?' he asked, looking straight ahead.

I passed it to him and he unscrewed the top and squirted a long jet into his mouth.

The two Americans stuck at it for a bit longer and then surrendered with apologies and those wholesome bleached smiles. The girls smiled back, then regrouped and carried on.

'If I could speak Spanish, Danny, I wouldn't hang around,' Simon said.

'Simon!' Fi said, reprimanding him in jest.

One of the girls – petite, with glossy black hair and stunning, brown eyes; eyes that would have nailed me to the floor and sent my pulse racing had they shone at me – was looking over at Billy. He didn't seem to notice as he lay back against the fence.

'Billy, you lucky sod,' Eddy said. 'I think one of them has the eye for you.'

'Is it enough of a challenge for him though?' Simon asked. 'I can't see any ring...' He closed his eyes and took a deep breath through his nose, as if he was forcing the unspoken, queued-up words back into his lungs.

'What did you say?' Billy asked him.

'Nothing,' he replied, eyes still closed, his breaths still deep.

'Come on. I don't know what you're trying to start here, but just spit it out.'

Simon opened his eyes and stared at him. 'How can you say I'm starting something? I think you're forgetting something, Billy. This is something you started, not me.'

'Simon!' Fi snapped. 'You promised me.'

He took a step back and held up his hands. 'I'm sorry,' he said, looking at Fi, then Billy. 'OK?'

The fiesta didn't let up. It was dark now and the air smelt of wine and cigars and perfumed sweat. And we kept drinking, but didn't dance. The two American boys that had tried to dance, that had tried to get in with the Spanish girls, were by the fence, next to Billy. They must have guessed Billy wasn't Spanish. One of them asked him in English if he was going to run.

'No,' he said, not bothering to look at them.

They weren't to be put off though. 'Oh, we are,' the taller one told him.

'Where are you from?' the other one asked him.

'San Francisco.'

'No kidding, man!'

'Yeah, we're studying in Berkeley,' the taller one added.

'So you doing Europe as well then?' his friend asked.

Billy turned to them, flat as you like. 'What do you mean, "doing"?' he asked.

'You know, travelling around.'

'No, my friend lives out here.' He nodded in my direction.

'Hi, nice to meet you,' the taller one said to me.

'You too.'

'You going to run then?' he asked.

'No way.'

'We are, aren't we, Tom?'

The shorter one nodded and smiled. 'Yeah, for sure. That's why we're here.'

These guys were too keen, too sure and complacent for their own good, and it irritated me. 'Well, you better be sure you know what you're doing.'

'Well, we've read *Fiesta*,' the taller one said, as if that was adequate preparation, as if it would somehow protect them. Two hundred and eighteen pages of book, with less than two on the encierro, against six half-ton bulls. Yes, they'd prepared properly for this one all right.

'Hasn't everyone?' Billy pointed out, and shook his head.

'Good luck,' I said. 'You might need it.'

The shorter one went all Tom Cruise on me, with a wink and a slick *Top Gun* smile. 'They say it's a cinch, man.'

'Do they now?' I asked. 'And who's they?'

'Some buddies of ours. Did it last year. They were telling us about it before we came out. Gotta have a few beers down you to give you a bit of spunk and then run like shit.' He seemed to like that one. He was laughing. He looked at his watch. 'Hey, Johnny we gotta get going.' He turned to us to explain. 'Meant to be meeting some friends at the fountain at half eleven. See you guys later. Nice to meet you.'

'You too,' I said.

Billy didn't acknowledge them as they walked off. 'Fucking idiots,' he said, to no one in particular.

'I don't know about you,' Eddy said. 'But I'm rather hungry.'

And so was everyone else. I'd forgotten about being hungry until food was mentioned. I was quite happy drinking. We didn't even bother trying to get into a restaurant for all the crowds, but instead chose a shop where we bought some French stick chorizo sandwiches and more wine to top up the bota. We sat outside on the kerb and set about our dinner. Fi couldn't manage all hers and gave it to a skinny stray dog that was hanging around in front of her.

'What's the time?' I asked Billy.

He looked at his Omega. 'Ten to twelve.'

'Hey, we should go down to the corrals and look at the bulls at some point,' I said to everyone.

At some point. Once we'd got a few more hours of fiesta under our belts.

Billy needed the toilet. So did I. The others waited for us back at the fenced-off bar where the Spanish girls were still dancing.

'Are you all right, Billy?' I asked, as we walked away from Estafeta, to try and find a less crowded bar where we could use the toilet. It was obvious Billy wasn't all right. He'd hardly said a word since the bar where the girls had danced paso dobles.

'No, I'm not. I just wish he would be straight about it. He keeps dropping comments here and there. "I can't see any ring".'

'I don't think it was a good idea you and Fi turning up together after the bullfight.'

'And why the hell not? Yeah, right. We had wild sex in the middle of the street, with a crowd watching on, if you want to know.'

'Well it obviously got the alarm bells ringing. And to be honest, Billy, I think I'd have felt the same way in his position.'

'But you're not in his position. And I don't think it's any of your fucking business to be taking sides.'

'I'm not taking sides. And anyway, it's fast becoming my business. Do you think I'd have got you all out here if I'd known?' He didn't answer, so I carried on. 'Of course I bloody wouldn't.'

He didn't seem to be listening. 'He must know. Why else would he have said it?'

'Maybe he was referring to Fi,' I pointed out. 'She's got a ring on her finger, as well. But why the fuck can't you just leave it for tonight?'

'Because I can't. I just want to know if he knows, that's all. Because I can't fucking stand these mind games, his comments. If she got divorced as a result, well, big deal, I'm sorry. I mean, half the fucking world's divorced, aren't they?'

And I realised Billy wouldn't let it drop until he found out. Even if it meant us all having a bad night of it. I despised his selfishness just then. 'Well, go on then. Why don't you just have it out with him? And apologise.'

'I don't think it's something I need to apologise about.'

'All right. OK. But at least just say it, even if you don't mean it.'

He looked at me for a moment, then nodded. 'Right, I'll apologise, if it makes you all feel better.'

And at the time it was the best I could hope for.

Once again we squeezed our way down Estafeta, which was really heaving and swaying now, and turned left past the lit-up Ayuntamiento. Just round the corner we suddenly ran out of fiesta. It was still and quiet and slightly eerie as we walked down the hill of Santo Domingo, to where they kept the bulls.

At the bottom, the road was cordoned off by a rope a few feet in front of a robust wooden fence on the left that you couldn't see over. Between the rope and the fence two policemen were sitting in their car, smoking. Up and away to our left, a group of people were looking across and down towards the fence. We climbed up the steps to get a look.

There was no mad fiesta up here, only our hushed voices talking in reverential tones, because even from this distance, high up and way out of danger, the bulls commanded respect. Just to see them was enough. Just to sense them. You couldn't see that much. Dark shapes and rough outlines. But you could hear them. Bells rang softly, and there was the occasional snort; you could feel their presence all right.

I thought there was a way we could get a better look at them, from round the other side, so we went back down the steps, crossed over the road and slipped under a fence further up from the bulls. Simon, Fi and I scaled a stone wall and crept along the grass verge directly above the corral.

Billy stayed behind with Eddy. Eddy wasn't too steady on his feet.

We were just a few yards away now but safe. Looking down on them, the first thing that struck me was their size. You could just make out the branded numbers on their flanks in the moonlight. And now we were close enough to hear them, the soft heave of their breathing as they dozed gave me the shivers. It masked their explosive menace. Until that moment, I had never fully appreciated the sheer proportions and magnificence of a bull and it sobered me up.

'They're incredible,' Fi whispered.

'Unbelievable,' Simon said.

I could scarcely hear Simon and Fi but the bulls and steers must have sensed us because they started to get restless. The bells round the steers' necks got louder. A car door slammed and seconds later, a torch shone our way.

'Bajaos de ahí!'

It was the police.

'I take it we're not meant to be up here,' Simon said.

'Let's get out of here,' I said.

We crawled back along the grass verge and were down the wall fast. We met Eddy and Billy back in the street. Eddy had his hands on his knees, looking down at the cobbled stone road.

'Is he all right?' Simon asked Billy.

'Yeah. Just had a bit much to drink.'

We waited a couple of minutes for Eddy to recover and then walked slowly back up the hill towards the Ayuntamiento. The hill – Santo Domingo – was where the real hard core started their run, right at the beginning where the bulls come charging out of the corral, dangerous in the extreme, as there's no obvious escape route. Just huge unclimbable stone walls on either side. In a few hours' time, this very same stretch of now silent street would be total mayhem as frantic runners dived out of the way of the stampeding bulls.

Fi took her straw hat off and fanned herself as we got to the top of Santo Domingo. It was a warm night. Too warm. The south wind hadn't let up.

And back on Estafeta the party was still thumping. People were singing and dancing and drinking, just as before. If anything it was even wilder now. And the bands just kept playing. A Scandinavian-looking guy was crashed out on the pavement, his T-shirt stained a patchy purple, a pool of fresh vomit a couple of feet to his left. A group of his friends were standing over him. One of them poured water on his face. The guy sat up briefly, not knowing where the hell he was by the look of him, and then lay back down and closed his eyes.

One of his friends bent down and shook his shoulder. 'Come on, Jurgen. The bull running isn't far away. You've got to sober up for that, mate,' he said.

'If he's going to run, I don't see why I shouldn't,' Eddy said, a picture of sobriety in comparison. 'In fact, I think we should all run.'

Billy looked at him hard. 'Have you got a death wish or something?'

'No. Of course I haven't.'

'Well, don't even think about it then.'

We stopped in a bar just off the Plaza del Castillo. Framed black and white photos of bullfights from a bygone era lined the walls. It was in need of fresh paint and fresh air. But it wasn't as full as other places, just a few old locals in there, smoking cigars and playing cards.

I got the drinks in – we were all tired of wine – and it was rum and Cokes all round. An old man in a beret was up at the bar, drinking a brandy.

'Hola,' I said.

'Hola. Qué tal?'

'Bien, gracias.'

He looked me in the eyes, which were red no doubt, from lack of sleep and too much wine. 'Oye, ten cuidado con los toros.'

'Sí, pero no vamos a correr. Pues, espero que no. Mi amigo sentado ahí, el chico gordo,' I said, pointing over at Eddy, 'quiere correr.'

The old man took one look at Eddy and shook his head. Then he walked over to the table where they were sitting and waved a thick finger at him. 'Que no corras, tío.'

Eddy looked at me up at the bar. 'What's he saying?'

'Not to run.'

'I didn't say I was definitely going to run. I'm just thinking about it, that's all.'

The old boy came back to the bar. 'Vamos a ver. Ha empinado el codo y no ha dormido, verdad?'

'Sí.'

'Entonces si corre, está loco.'

He went on to explain what Eddy should do if he was stupid enough to run. I thanked him then brought the drinks over and sat down. I looked at a framed photo of a bullfighter in action on the wall next to us. It was signed. There was a crack in the glass.

'What did that guy say to you at the bar?' Eddy asked.

'Said that if you've been drinking and had no sleep, you'd be crazy to run. But if you're stupid enough to run and you fall, stay down and cover your head. Whatever you do, don't try and get up. And if you're on Estafeta when they reach you, don't try and hide in the doorways.'

'Yes, come on, Eddy,' Simon said. 'Take his word for it. Let's just watch it. I'm sure he knows what he's talking about. He's probably seen more encierros than you've had gourmet dinners.'

Eddy had his elbows on the table and rubbed his forehead with the tips of his fingers. He drank some rum and Coke and smiled. 'It's nice to know you're all so concerned about me.' Then he stopped smiling. 'But why is it no one ever takes me seriously? I'm fed up of being taken as a joke. Just because I'm overweight, doesn't mean to say I'm incapable of running,' he said.

'It's nothing to do with your weight, Eddy. I know you're perfectly capable of running,' I told him. 'It's just that you've drunk too much.'

He looked up at the matador on the wall. 'Rubbish.'

I was keen we all drank quickly, to try and get Eddy pissed enough so he wouldn't be able to run; I'd heard the police weren't meant to let the seriously drunk run. I don't know if Simon was thinking the same but he got another round in as soon as we'd finished the first ones. And by the end of it Eddy was dozing, or so it seemed, the side of his face resting on the drink-stained sticky table top. I did a thumbs up at Simon, as if to say 'mission accomplished', and he smiled back.

Billy was frowning, not paying any attention to our efforts at stopping Eddy from running. It was as if the world around him was completely eclipsed by whatever was crossing his mind.

'Are you still with us, Billy?' Simon asked.

Billy cleared his throat. 'Yeah.' He looked up at Simon. 'Hey, I just want to say I'm… I'm sorry.'

'For what?'

'I think you know.'

'No. What exactly for, Billy?'

'Oh come on. Stop playing games with me.'

Simon sipped on his rum and Coke, put his glass carefully back on the table, all the time looking at Billy. 'OK. So are you referring to my mother, or something else?'

Billy looked up at the ceiling and the flaking paint. 'Your mother,' he said. 'But I want you to know, it never meant that much to me.'

'Oh great, that's great to know.'

'No, I'm just trying to say it wasn't that serious, that's all.'

'Bit of fun then, was it? That's even better,' Simon said. Eddy opened his drained eyes, life creeping back into them, and sat up. 'You know,' Simon continued. 'I think we need to talk about it properly. Give my mother that respect at least. We need to sit down and work our way through this. With a fine-tooth comb.'

Fi grabbed Simon's wrist. 'Not now, though, please.'

'What do you take me for, Fi?! I had absolutely no intention of talking about it now.'

'No, I know you didn't.'

'Then why the hell did you say it then?' He took a deep breath and looked at Billy again. 'We'll talk about this after the fiesta. And I'm going outside for a moment.'

He got up and left the bar.

'Excuse me a moment as well,' Fi said, getting up, and then hurrying out after him.

'What was all that about?' Eddy asked.

'Oh, I don't know,' Billy said.

Eddy yawned. 'I guess it still must be very raw. Still getting over the whole thing. Mind you, I think he's coped remarkably well, considering. It was absolutely horrendous, wasn't it?'

'Am I missing something here?' Billy asked. His eyes narrowed in on Eddy.

'What do you mean?'

'Well, do you know something I don't?'

'What? About his parents?'

'Yeah.' Billy reached for my cigarettes and lit one. His hand was shaking slightly.

'Don't you know?!' Eddy asked. He didn't sound so much surprised as astonished.

'No.'

'God, I thought the whole world knew.'

'Well tell me, for fuck's sake, will you?!'

Eddy didn't seem to catch Billy's agitation. 'I just can't believe you don't know. His father killed her. About three years ago now. It was even in the papers. Shot her in the head with a twelve-bore shotgun down in Cornwall. After she'd gone to bed.'

There had to be a mistake. I must have heard him wrong or something. Then as I looked at those red eyes, not drunk now but fully alive and dead serious, I was smacked in the face by a fact. This was no mistake. It was true. 'Oh Christ,' I said.

'Tell me you're lying, Eddy.'

'No. Why would I lie about it?'

'Please tell me you're fucking lying!'

'No, of course I'm not.'

Billy stood up and gritted his teeth before bringing his fist down on the table top. Drinks went everywhere. Locals looked round.

'I need some fresh air,' he said. He started walking towards the door.

'Billy!' I shouted.

'Just leave me alone for a bit, OK?' he said, without turning round, all emotion bled, like a slit throat, from his voice.

I was about to run out after him but I didn't. I knew he would need some time and space to sort out the pieces after that explosive bit of news. Once he'd gone though, I remember thinking that it could take months, years, possibly a lifetime of time and space to get over the shell-shock and shrapnel wounds. And the same for Simon. And maybe they both never would. Maybe they'd die with their scars not properly healed.

And I remember thinking Simon was right after all, the poor bastard. So he really did know about shooting. More than anyone should ever have to know.

I saw his father climb those narrow stairs, shotgun in hand, and open the bedroom door. I saw him lift the gun up and point it at her. I just hope she was asleep and not sitting up reading. And I could see her blood and bits of brain splashed right across the back wall like a Jackson Pollock painting. I felt sick.

'Did I say something wrong?' Eddy asked, smiling awkwardly at me, for reassurance probably.

I really didn't want to go through the whole sordid, bloody mess again. Not just then. He'd find out sooner or later. 'No,' I said. 'Nothing. What do you want to drink?'

'Same again, please, Dan.'

And so I got up, picked up what mess I could off the floor, and then took it up to the bar and put it in the bin, before ordering two very large drinks.

Eddy had a sip on the very large rum and Coke I brought back. 'I think I'm going to run, Dan,' he said.

A moment later, a group of four young American boys came in. They looked like students 'doing Europe'. They were on their toes and looked about the bar with clear eyes. These boys were definitely going to run.

An hour went by and there was still no sign of Billy. Nor Simon or Fi either. I decided it was time to go and look for

Billy. Eddy was now flexing his leg muscles, mimicking the Americans, who were still up at the bar and looking far less white-eyed now.

'I'm going off to try and find Billy. I'll see you back here in a bit,' I said. 'Whatever you do, please don't run. If we lose each other, I'll meet you back at the car.'

It was starting to get light outside. The party mood had died down, replaced by anticipation. The encierro was less than an hour and a half away. Young fresh faced 'mozos' were starting to appear. These boys had slept and these boys were ready. Their white T-shirts and red handkerchiefs and sashes were clean and they had the morning papers in their hands, which they would use to wave in front of the bulls as a diversionary tactic. It's supposed to deflect attention away from the runner and on to the paper, and the bull will go for the paper, instead of them. That's the theory, at least. There were plenty of up-all-nighters amongst them, getting ready. A bleary-eyed Australian lad stopped me at the bullring end of Estafeta to finalise his preparations.

'Which way do the bulls come from?' he asked.

I pointed in the opposite direction to the bullring, kept my finger straight down Estafeta and then bent it round past the Ayuntamiento. 'That way,' I said.

He thanked me, and then staggered off down Estafeta.

I couldn't find Billy. With so many people about, there was very little chance. I was about to go back to the bar when it came to me where he might be. The Hemingway statue. My hunch proved right. He was sitting at the base of the statue. I sat down next to him.

'Shit, I'm sorry, Billy.'

He sighed deeply, then looked skyward. 'I just can't believe she's dead.'

'Neither can I.'

'I mean a divorce, OK. But he fucking shot her,' he said, shaking his head.

I saw that mottled, red wall again and wondered if it might have had something to do with Billy after all. 'It was nothing to do with you though, Billy. It happened a long time after.'

He didn't seem to be listening, as if he was in a trance. 'And to think I used that twelve-bore. I fired it loads of times. We had so much fun with it as well. We couldn't wait to the evening to blast rabbits with it.'

I think he was getting at the irony of it. Anyway, I certainly wasn't going to point it out to him. I couldn't think of anything to say so I just passed him the bota. I thought it would do him good and he drank deeply. Hopefully it would make him forget for a little, take the edge off it a bit. Anything to take his mind off what he'd just heard.

'I just want to be alone for a bit,' he said.

'Sure.' I put my arm round him. 'Look, I'll be back at that bar. If we're not in there, we'll be watching from around over there, I imagine.' I pointed to a spot about twenty yards away, on the curve, looking down Estafeta one way, and towards the bullring in the other direction. 'If we don't meet up, you know where the car is, don't you?'

'Yeah.'

159

'We'll probably be in the bar for another half an hour or so.'

'See you,' he said.

As I walked back to the bar, my head was a mess. The poor bastards. The pair of them. Inside, I saw Simon at the bar, buying drinks. Eddy was still sitting at the table. I couldn't see Fi.

'Where's Fi?' I asked, when he returned with two cuba libres.

'We had a bit of a disagreement. I told her I've changed my mind. And she went off in a huff.'

'Changed your mind about what?'

He sipped his cuba libre, swirled the ice around his glass. 'I've decided I'm going to run.'

'Are you crazy?'

'No, I'm not. And Billy? Where's he? Not with Fi again, is he?'

'No.'

'And I'm meant to believe you this time, am I?'

'Yeah, I'm telling you the truth. He's sitting alone by the Hemingway statue if you really want to know, at least he was when I left him.'

They didn't finish their drinks. Simon stood up and summoned Eddy. 'Right, come on. Let's go and get him.'

'Yeah, come on, Dan. Don't be such a blouse. It'll be a laugh,' Eddy said.

'It'll be dangerous, Eddy, very dangerous. And besides, Billy won't run either. He can't run. Not with that leg of his.'

'It can't be that bad. I think we'll be able to persuade him,' Simon said.

'I'm certain we will,' Eddy said, before going off to the toilet.

'You know, I really hope this isn't something you feel you need to prove to him, Simon, because if it is –'

'No, of course it isn't,' he said, cutting my opinion clean off, and adding his own in the process. 'You sound just like Fi. I've got nothing to prove to him. Absolutely nothing.'

'Well, go on then,' I said, when Eddy returned and stood by the table. He looked keen to get going, awake now, and fidgety. 'Fuck off and run if that's what you really want to do. I'll meet you all by the statue, when it's over. But I think you're fucking nuts, you know? The pair of you.'

'Don't you at least want to watch us?' Eddy asked.

'No, I fucking don't!'

Eddy stood at the threshold and turned round. 'Are you sure, Dan?'

'Yes. Now just fuck off! And be bloody careful.'

The old man who'd advised Eddy against running was still up at the bar. He looked at me and shook his head, like he knew what they'd decided to do.

'Son idiotas,' I said.

'Que sí.'

I ordered a whisky to calm my nerves and a brandy for the old man, too.

I headed for the place where I told Billy I'd be. I hoped he'd had the sense to refuse. But Billy wasn't there. The police

161

were clearing the street of revellers. Officials slotted sturdy wooden planks into position to make the fences and block off the roads. There were two rows of wooden fences, with gaps between the horizontal slats, big enough for runners to get under or through and out of danger, but small enough to prevent the bulls following. The public weren't allowed past the back fence. And in the space between the two fences, the Red Cross waited with stretchers, ready for the accidents.

I perched myself up on the fence. It was solid with spectators. More officials swept the streets, clearing it of all the drink and food and occasional patches of vomit that had been spilt the night before. A man with a wheelbarrow followed them and sprinkled sawdust on the wet patches. I was watching from that notorious bottleneck where many a runner had been gored as the street narrows to the entrance to the ring.

I thought about the serious nutters getting into position now at the bottom of the hill on Santo Domingo, near the corrals, with just a few yards' start on the bulls. And the slightly saner, crowded at the Ayuntamiento, where they must have had a good 300-yard start. But even with that advantage there's no way anyone can get to the ring before the bulls. I'm told they run at almost twenty miles an hour. The only place where you can get into the ring safely without being caught is from the telecom building onwards. You've only got about ninety yards to run. The whole of Pamplona was clock-watching now. It was fast approaching eight o'clock.

I wondered where they'd decided to start from, and whether Billy was with them. It crossed my mind he might have gone off somewhere before they went off to get him.

Then at eight o'clock on the dot a rocket went off and all past and future vanished. The corral gates had been opened. Then another rocket went off seconds later, to tell Pamplona the bulls were out and on their way; that they were coming to get them. The runners who started at the telecom building soon came jogging by. They were booed and jeered at by the watching public as they made their way into the ring. They weren't really risking anything.

Moments later, others came running, closely followed by frantic sprinters, and on their heels the first of the bulls. Runners dived on both sides to get out of their way, the same way a bus's tyres sends water flying either side as it cuts through a flooded street. Mixed in were more runners. Someone fell. Everyone fell. There was chaos. A bull was having a field day amongst the fallen, tossing its head wildly into the heap of screaming bodies. But seconds later the bull was on its way again, thanks to a brave mozo who managed to distract it with his newspaper. Right in front of me a runner turned his head and saw a bull almost on him. He dived on the cobbles and scrambled under the slat of the fence. The Red Cross went to help him, but before they could get to him he was back under the fence and running again. It was all over in seconds.

I waited for what I thought was the sixth and final bull to go past, along with all the steers, and then got under the fence to follow them into the ring. It was only a twenty-yard run and you can get into the ring free that way, so I'd been told, provided you're not too late after them and get there before they close the gates. We jogged along gently, almost strolled really, until someone shouted, 'Todavía queda uno!'

I looked round and there it was. A loose bull not far behind us. I couldn't tell exactly how far but I'd say about fifteen yards or so – I just saw its horns and black forehead before I really started to run – and at that point it was everyone for themselves. Nowhere more so than in the narrow tunnel leading into the ring where there was absolutely no escape. People shoved and jostled frantically to get out. It seemed like both seconds and a lifetime before we emerged from the darkness and into the ring. The place was packed with runners and I clambered over the circular fence round the ring as fast as I could, nothing else on my mind than what was behind me. My heart thumped against my ribs like a madman banging on the bars of his cage as I finally caught my breath, hands on knees. Then I looked up.

I see Hemingway on the balcony of the Ayuntamiento, watching on. Watching on in spirit, with an empty glass in hand. At exactly the moment I look up and see the bull, he can't see that much, there's too much commotion for that, but he can hear the ambulance sirens get louder and louder. At one point he gets a glimpse of the plump, short-haired girl from the Red Cross holding a man's hand, squeezing it, reassuring him that he's going to be all right as she checks his pulse, while others try desperately to stem the flow of blood that is starting to form thin streams in the gaps between the cobbles. But that's all he sees. All I see is red.

The loose bull was in the ring now and causing real panic for those close enough to it. Taunted, goaded, disorientated, it turned, it swung round, it charged at men or boys either brave, mad or unlucky enough to get its attention.

'Shit, it's got blood on its right horn,' a flour-faced Englishman said, standing next to me and looking through a pair of binoculars, right up by the barrier, on the safe side. I thought he was talking to me.

Finally the bull found its way into the corral with the help of a steer. Then a rocket went up to tell the world that all the bulls were out of the ring and in the pen under the stands.

There were no sleepy faces now. Torrents of adrenalin made sure of that. Some runners were still panting a bit, others had got their breath back and stood composed, but every runner in the ring, down to the last, was wide-eyed alive.

Groups split up by the bulls were busy reforming. There was relief and smiles all round. Some American boys by the fence were recounting their tales of near horns eagerly to each other. They hugged and slapped each other on the back. It was the stuff of legends, like the ultimate rites of passage to manhood successfully negotiated which they'd surely write home about. What else was there to prove? They could relax now and get through their lives with the knowledge they'd passed the exam. They could even become accountants or actuaries for the next fifty years, smug with the knowledge they had graduated with honours from the Hemingway School of Pure Adventure. And no one could ever take that certificate away from them.

One of the American boys asked me to take a photo of them, which I did. They put their arms over each other's shoulders. They all looked so radiant. The kind of photo to show their grandchildren, I remember thinking.

Soon after, a heifer with taped-up horns was set loose amongst the crowd into the ring. It caught someone trying to act out the part of the matador and threw him into the air. Cheers went up. More heifers were released. More runners fancied themselves as amateur matadors, trying and failing with their crude, grotesque attempts to imitate the poised choreography of the professional.

'God, you should have seen it. It just went straight in under his ribs,' I overheard a mozo telling a group of four in Spanish, all immaculately dressed in pristine white, red scarf and sash round neck and waist.

'Qué pasó?' I butted in.

'A young lad was caught by a bull,' he told me. 'That last bull that came into the ring.'

'Where?'

'By the Ayuntamiento.' He turned to his companions again. 'And the strange thing was, he didn't even start running. He just pushed someone out of the way then turned round and faced them. A complete lunatic. Or a clown.'

'A foreigner?' one of his friends asked.

'What do you think? Of course. They shouldn't let those foreigners run. No tienen ni puta idea.'

I looked around and couldn't see them. Then I left the ring. None of them were by the Hemingway statue where we'd arranged to meet. I headed for the Ayuntamiento.

Estafeta was alive with the sounds of bumpy rise and bang of shutters, revealing empty bars about to open up and slake the thirst of that huge beast called San Fermín. It was business as usual.

It was Eddy. I sensed it. I knew I should have stopped him from running, and I was disgusted with myself. I saw a tragedy in that jovial laugh of his, those happy cheeks. It was something, I felt, that was destined to happen. I stopped and leant against a door. I started to sweat, and sweat cold. My chest turned wet, dampening my T-shirt. I took some deep breaths and tried to tell myself it could have been anyone, with so many foreigners running. I repeated the words, 'it could have been anyone', as if it were a mantra, as if it would convince me. Only then did I carry on walking.

Outside the Ayuntamiento, a buggy was scrubbing the cobbles. The driver kept running it over the same patch, four, five times. Two policemen looked on in silence. Three official-looking men in dark suits stood watching the cleaning from the balcony of the Ayuntamiento. One of them pointed to the flags flying from the building, and the other two nodded. They all went inside.

167

A handful of people watched the proceedings by the slatted wooden fence. And inside, on the road, stood a lone woman.

'Are you all right?' I asked her.

Fi looked across at me. 'Yes, just about. There was so much blood on the road. It was horrendous. Poor guy. Where are the others?'

'I don't know,' I said.

Just down from the policemen, a Red Cross volunteer started to kick the wooden fence and slam his fists into the highest railing. He was screaming, shouting obscenities, calling God a son of a whore, telling Him he'd shit on His whore of a mother. A woman, also Red Cross, tried to console him. He stopped, buried his head in her shoulder, shook violently.

'Did you see it happen?' I asked Fi.

'No. I just saw an ambulance go by further up. It must've been really serious.'

It could have been anyone, I told myself again. Absolutely anyone. 'It had to be a foreigner, didn't it? Always bloody foreigners. They just think it's a laugh.'

'How do you know it was a foreigner?'

'Someone in the ring told me.'

'Oh my God.' She put her hand to her mouth and lost her balance slightly.

I put my arm round her. Propping her up, trying to comfort her. 'Look. I'm sure he's fine. There are hundreds of foreigners that run. Anyway we said we'd meet them by the Hemingway statue. They're probably there right now.'

We waited by the statue for what seemed like ages, scanning faces. I paced around smoking, looking. Fi had started to shake, although it wasn't cold. Far from it. It was July and the south wind was waking up again.

'They're probably getting drunk somewhere,' I said, not that convinced, putting my arm round her once more and rubbing the top of hers. Comforting her, I thought.

'I'd have thought so.' She didn't sound convinced either, although I could tell she wanted to be. 'Or maybe they found somewhere to get a bit of sleep.'

'Maybe.'

A few minutes later I was back to pacing, smoking another. 'Fi, Eddy told us both what happened to Simon's mother. I'm really sorry.'

'Oh God, he didn't, did he?'

'Yes. I think he thought we both knew.'

'Well maybe they're talking it over somewhere.'

'That's right.' I trod on the butt and lit a fresh one. 'Hey, Fi,' I finally said.

'What?'

'Maybe we should try the hospital.'

It was something I reckon that had crossed both our minds at some point but neither of us wanted to voice it, and let it develop into a viable possibility. 'Maybe they're in the bar', 'maybe they've found a place to sleep', 'maybe they're talking things over'. These 'maybes' were our made-up defences to shield us from thinking the worst. But as we stood by the statue for those silent few seconds, the more reassuring possibilities seemed to shrink and wither in front of the one 'maybe' we didn't want to contemplate.

I remember seeing a lot of people milling about in the reception area. And I remember noticing some of them had pens and notepads in their hands as I made my way through them all to the desk. I can't remember if it was a man or a woman I asked but I remember not hearing their answer. What I will never forget, though, was seeing Eddy sat on a bench on my right, shaking uncontrollably, with Simon sitting next to him, head in his hands. Both their T-shirts were now more liver brown/red than white. The unmistakeable sight of dried blood. The backs of Simon's fingers were caked in it.

And then Eddy's words as I looked at his drained face, into his red eyes. 'I'm sorry, Dan. I'm so fucking sorry.'

'What have you done, Eddy?'

'I didn't.'

He started to sob and covered his face with hands.

'You didn't what?'

'We couldn't stop him. We couldn't.'

My chest went very tight and I struggled for breath. 'Where's Billy?'

He didn't answer.

'Where's Billy, Eddy?!' I grabbed his shoulders and shook him.

He looked at me, his face a wet, puffed-up mess. 'A bull caught him. They couldn't stop the bleeding.'

After that I can remember letting go of him and looking

towards the reception desk. I remember journalists looking on, scribbling. Then for the first time in my life, I totally lost it. I stood up and ran at the nearest one, punching out wildly. 'Go on, vete a la mierda! Hijo de puta!'

I got him on the floor and laid into him with my fists, with all I had. I was smashing his eye out, blinding the bastard with my knuckles, as they pulled me off. Then it all went black.

The next thing I remember was waking in a hospital bed. Eddy was sitting in a chair beside me. I wondered why my right hand ached. I could only just move my fingers. My knuckles were red and swollen. I looked at them for a few seconds and then at Eddy's long face. I remembered now.

'How did it happen?'

Eddy looked down at the floor, then back at me. 'We couldn't stop him, Dan. I swear. We were all set to run at the town hall, there.' He looked down at the floor again. 'Then as the bulls rounded the bend at the top of the hill, he pushed Simon out of the way and turned round and faced them. I screamed at him to get out of the way but he just stood there, shouted back something about liking it dangerous. And one of them caught him.' He looked me right in the eye. 'There was nothing we could do, Dan. I promise. It all happened so fast.'

I didn't say anything. There was nothing to say. I just kept picturing him turning to face the oncoming herd. I couldn't believe he was dead. It just wouldn't register. I expected him to come through the door at any moment, to defy the facts, because Billy couldn't die. He was immortal.

Later on that day, Simon and Fi came to see me. Fi asked me if I was OK, a stupid question really but the most compassionate question anyone could ask in the circumstances and I was grateful she asked. Simon said how sorry he was and asked me if there was anything I needed. I told him there was nothing. They left the room and then Simon returned a few minutes later. He sat in the chair next to the bed.

'I hope you believe me when I tell you I didn't want this to happen.' I didn't answer. 'I didn't, Dan. Yes, he made me angry, and resentful, but I didn't want him to die. What I really wanted was an opportunity to talk things through with him, but he never gave me that chance. There were just too many things that got in the way. He didn't make it easy for me.'

'I know,' I said.

'I blame Billy for a lot of things, Dan, but I don't blame him for my mother's death and the selfish bastard never gave me the chance to tell him that.'

I was desperate to blame someone, anyone. The Red Cross, the doctors, for not saving him. Eddy, for wanting to run in the first place. Simon, for persuading him to run and having a mother who could seduce him. And myself, of course, for getting them all out here together on holiday in the first place. I wanted to blame someone. But the blame just wouldn't stick.

It kept shifting back onto Billy, and his selfishness. What he did could never have brought Simon's mother back. But by ending his own personal suffering, all he had achieved was to add more bloody drops to life's grim pool of misery. It made me wonder how much he really feared the consequences for those left behind. Or was he more frightened of his own long-term pain? It also made me realise that perhaps I never really knew him. I couldn't decide whether what he'd done was brave or cowardly, and I'd never known the coward in Billy. I could only see it in myself.

The American Consulate in Bilbao broke the news to his parents, waking them in the middle of the night with a phone call. It must have been awful for them hearing that phone ring. The act of waking, half-conscious, and then a split second later, that sudden lucid grim awareness that what awaited them on the other end of the line could only be bad, that calls at that time of the night almost always spelt tragic news.

His body was taken to Pamplona airport, where his parents were waiting to take him home, via Madrid. We met briefly, for the first time. His mother looked worn out, understandably – thick crescent-moon bags under bloodshot eyes, no doubt a result of the tragedy and the long-haul flight. His father wasn't so expressive. Like Billy, he didn't give much away.

I didn't know what to say. I couldn't really wish them a good flight back, not with them being fully aware that for a good twelve hours they'd be flying across the Atlantic with their dead, boxed-up son just a few feet below them. Eddy, Fi and Simon didn't say much either.

'He always spoke very well of you,' his mother told me, as we reached the departure gate. And then she put her hand into her pocket and pulled out his Omega watch. 'We were going through his things last night and we came across this. We'd like you to have it.'

'Thank you,' I said.

I took it from her outstretched hand and for a moment I didn't know what to do with it. I ended up putting it very carefully into the front pocket of my dirty, crumpled jeans.

She stepped forward and hugged me.

I took a deep breath and tried to hold it as best I could, before letting it out slowly. I just managed to hold myself together. Just. 'God, I'm sorry,' I said.

She broke down in tears.

And then we finally separated and they disappeared through passport control, towards what was bound to be a long, very difficult journey. A journey that would probably last a lifetime.

I said goodbye to the others outside the terminal building.

Fi hugged me hard, very hard.

Simon did the same. He looked close to tears, tilting his head back as if to stop them spilling over the edge.

Then Eddy put his arms round me. He looked awful. And two slow tears crept out. He wiped them away with the back of his hand and sniffed hard.

'You weren't to know, Eddy. Don't be too hard on yourself, hey?'

'No, nor you either.'

'See you,' I said.

And then I found the car park, sat in the Fiat and didn't put the keys in the ignition until the downpour stopped. My downpour. Twenty minutes later, I left for Santander. Simon, Fi and Eddy left that afternoon as well, on the British Airways flight out of Bilbao to Heathrow.

I didn't see it. I was at the other end of Estafeta when it happened. And yet I saw it all. From my hospital bed, I saw it on just about every news bulletin that day. One even had a slow-motion replay, with one of those bright circles round Billy, to highlight his death. And I saw all the stills on the front page of every paper the following day. *ABC* even had it in colour, taking up the whole front page, and you could just about make out the flecks of blood spraying out of his side as the right horn went in and tossed him into the air. And inside *El País* on page 37, I saw possibly the last printed image of Billy alive, on his knees, cheeks inflated like a balloon as the last wind burst out of him seconds after impact, left hand raised like he'd finally surrendered.

I saw it all. And not just from television and photos either, but from printed words as well. Him instinctively trying to stand up and collapsing straight away. Unstoppable blood pumping out of him, 90 per cent of it gone in the eight minutes it took from the horning to getting him to hospital by ambulance. I saw the defeated, worn-out faces of the surgeons after forty-one frantic minutes in the operating theatre, where they must have known from the start that they didn't stand a chance, given what the head of Emergency was quoted as saying, that in over thirty years there, he'd never seen an injury so serious. And lastly, I saw the sad shake of the head from the witness who put it down to daring high spirits. To Hemingway, he supposed.

This time there was no morbid curiosity, no life lust, as I scoured the news for details. There was just a dull pain in my gut and an overload of aching, queasy head. But I needed to make sense of it. I needed to see it to believe it. And I saw it all.

I saw more than I wanted. Much more, for weeks after. I saw him mustering up the final resolve to turn round and face them, and Eddy's screaming horror. At times I saw the electrifying speed of the violence, at other moments the slow choreography of it all, like a shooting in a Peckinpah Western, like a death at the opera. And I saw it everywhere. On the huge cut-out bulls that advertise Osborne brandy on hills in sight of major roads out of towns. On the beach, watching kids kick a ball about. On smiling faces in packed bars. On the back of my eyelids in the dead of night.

I can hardly begin to imagine what Simon must have seen, how many times that night must have played through his head. He'd have had to go through it all again as well, at his father's trial. He'd have known whether there were signs of alcohol in his father's blood, the exact time she was ripped apart, the precise medical definitions of the injuries suffered to her face and head. Maybe he had to see her in the morgue to testify it was her, or maybe her injuries were so bad that what was left of her face resembled a butcher's bin more than a human being, and they wouldn't let him see her. He would have had to deal with what he felt for his father – and I'm sure, is still doing so. He might even have known whether she was awake or asleep as his father came into the room and pointed those two barrels at her. I just hope for Simon's sake and hers, she was asleep. And he would have known if his father's barrister cited her affair with Billy in his defence.

But amongst all those grim, death-filled possibilities, one beautiful fact survived. Simon had said it wasn't Billy's fault. And even if he didn't believe it, or even if he was trying to squash his gut feeling, it was an incredibly big thing to say.

I sent him a letter, telling him how sorry I was about his mother, how sorry I was for everything. I told him I was with him, that he could always count on me.

He wrote back, thanking me for my sympathy. He was with me too, all the way. And he told me to look after myself.

WEEKS AFTER PAMPLONA

I ended up in hospital again. Everything felt cold and empty and blue then black after I got back to Santander, and I got into drinking seriously for a good three months after – my way of committing temporary suicide, a shrink would probably tell you – and I ended up having my stomach pumped. A few friends came to see me, especially Enara. She was the one who found me. Apparently they had to break my door down to get in. Found me on the floor of my cockroached toilet, two empty bottles of whisky by my side.

My mother came out to see me as well, with a 'get well soon' card from my father, apologising for not being able to make it. He was being treated for an ear infection and had been advised by his doctor not to fly. I wondered if the treatment would make him listen a bit more. I doubted it though. His parting words of wisdom were straight from the pulpit. 'As your grandfather used to say, "Drink's a great friend but a bad master".' As if I, of all people, didn't know that! The stupid old fool! Still, it was nice of him to send a card.

And just before my mother left to go back to her hotel that night, she broke the news that my brother and Lisa were coming out to see me with their baby boy, my nephew. I flatly refused to see them at first but, as mothers do, she managed to persuade me it would be for the best.

Throughout the next day though, the day before they arrived, I struggled with the idea. While I genuinely wanted to put it all behind us, I also had a heartfelt desire to spit in their faces. And I resented the fact that they wanted to visit me in hospital – and see me at my weakest.

I smiled at them both as they walked in, too done in to fight. Physically, Lisa hadn't changed much. Her hair was slightly shorter and motherhood had rounded her a bit. But what struck me most was that there was now a beautiful glow about her, a perfect, composed pride – the type of pride, I imagine, that only recent mothers with their firstborn will ever know. My brother was turning slightly grey.

'You're both looking well,' I said, knowing it wasn't exactly a compliment they could repay. And it made me feel better.

'Thanks,' she said.

'We brought you these. It's not much, but it's what Mum said you missed most about England.' My brother handed me a bag. I looked inside and saw two pots of Marmite and three big boxes of tea bags. There was also a Lonely Planet book in there, *Trekking in Spain.*

'That's very nice of you.' I opened the book and noticed they'd written in it. 'Happy walking,' it said. 'Love always, Lisa, Rob and Luke.'

I smiled and looked down at a blond little bundle in a pushchair. He was waving his tiny arms by his sides, propeller-like. 'So you're Luke then?' I asked.

He stopped and stared at me, fascinated, confused, with

a look that suggested he was either about to cry or to smile. I made faces at him, crossed my eyes, stuck my tongue out. He began to smile and started waving his arms again, ready for take-off.

'Yes, this is Luke. My naughty little Luke,' Lisa said, as she unstrapped him from his pushchair, blew a great fart of a kiss into his neck, then put him on the bed. 'Luke William.'

'Hello, Luke. Luke William.' I lifted him up and kissed his pink little forehead. He looked around for his mum, with anxious little eyes, and she stretched out her arm. Luke grabbed her hand and then started to pull at her watch strap.

'He's got a thing about watches. They fascinate him. Especially ones with second hands.'

I thought about it for a few seconds as he tugged on his mother's strap.

'I've got something for him,' I said. 'It doesn't have a second hand though.'

I reached across to the bedside table and picked up the Omega. I handed it to Luke. He touched it, held it, dropped it on the bed and I picked it up again and gave it to his mother.

'Give it to him when he's older,' I said. 'It means a lot to me.'

'It's beautiful,' she said, looking at its face.

'I know. It was Billy's.'

Luke William was a sweet little thing and as I bounced him up and down on my stomach and watched him smile at me and make happy noises, I started to cry. Rob squeezed my shoulder and left the room. That was good of him, I suppose. Lisa sat on the bed and hugged me.

'It's all right,' she said. 'Let it all out. Go on. It's going to be OK.'

It was something I had to do. The day after I left hospital, we took the local ferry across the bay and walked all the way to the far end of a very cold and windy beach in Somo. We sat, wrapped up, on a rock and watched a handful of surfers crawl out, ride back in.

'You know that night, Enara… up on the hill?'

'Yes?'

'I just want to say I'm sorry.'

'You don't have to.'

A huge wave unrolled. A couple of surfers caught it.

'And also, I didn't go with a… with a prostitute.'

'No?'

'No.'

'I thought you had.'

'Well, I didn't.' I looked across the bay at Santander. The big ferry back to England was heading out. Its wake rocked a fishing boat coming back in.

'There's something you need to know,' I said. 'I mean, you've been really good to me and I think I… I can't fight much more.'

'Fight what?'

'Well… things.' And then I said it. 'Feelings, I suppose.'

She turned away from the surfers and smiled. She shook

her head, still smiling at me, and ruffled my hair. 'Come on,' she said. 'It's cold out here. Let's go.'

I've stopped drinking. It hasn't been easy, walking past all the bars full of old, familiar voices, calling me back in. I'll have a grape juice with them, but it's not the same. They'll sometimes tempt me with a beer and I'll decline and say I have to go. It feels lonelier without my 'friend', but that's the great paradox and attraction of drink for you. The way it relieves and shields you from the very state it creates – and for me, alcoholism's the loneliest state of all. But I do feel better for stopping. Better during the day, at least.

Enara's moving in next month. Into the spare room. Only temporarily, I hope. I don't want her in there forever. It just wouldn't work. At some point I want her out – out of that room and into mine. And now I'm sober, I know – as far as I can – that I want to be with her. I also know it's still very much in me to ruin it all with drink again, and always will be. It frightens me, haunts my new dreams, but I have to live with that, keep reminding myself. At the moment, it's a price well worth paying. And I pray I'll always feel that way.

She's been wonderful. So supportive. We've just got back from a ten-day trip down south, to Ronda. An old school friend of hers lives down there and Enara thought it would be good for me to get away for a bit and clear my head. We also did some walking in the foothills of the Sierra Nevada. It's a spectacular town, Ronda. High up on that plateau and split in half by a gorge with sheer drops of up to 400 feet by the bridge. And the views across the plains to the mountains are magnificent. They say Hemingway imagined Ronda for the scene in *For Whom The Bell Tolls*, where Republicans marched Nationalist soldiers across the square of the Ayuntamiento and pushed them over the edge of the cliff to their death.

I had to see the bullring, the famous ring. I had to try and lay the ghost to rest. The museum next to the ring is good although it got to me after a while and I had to leave. Photos of Hemingway – I couldn't get away from him – and Orson Welles watching the bullfights and plenty of gruesome reminders that the bull occasionally won.

Winter's here now and there's fresh snow on the mountains. My mother phoned the other day to see how I was. She wants me to go back to England and enrol with a shrink, but I don't know. I'm not sure I want to dig it all up again. It's too late to find a teaching job in an Academy, not that I would have done it. The prospect of teaching again doesn't really appeal to me just now. To be honest, I don't really know what does. I have days when it gets bad and other days when it gets worse and then occasionally, just occasionally, I wish it had been me and not Billy. But those are the blackest moments, the worst. On good days, I'm just grateful to be alive, with a chance of getting close again.

ABOUT THE AUTHOR

Andy Rumbold was born in London. After graduating from Birmingham University, he decided to spend six months in northern Spain, but stayed for four and a half years. He is now back in England, teaching English and Spanish at a school in Surrey, and working on his second novel.

The Last Fiesta was shortlisted for the Long Barn Books First Novel Award, judged by novelist Susan Hill.